SUPPORTING ACT

Agnes Lidbeck

Translated by
Nichola Smalley

PEIRENE

First published in Great Britain in 2025 by
Peirene Press Ltd
The Studio
10 Palace Yard Mews
Bath BA1 2NH
www.peirenepress.com

Published by agreement with Brave New World Agency

This translation © Nichola Smalley, 2025

ISBN 978-1-916806-08-5

Designed by Orlando Lloyd
Cover image © Gerhard Richter 2024 (0156)
Typeset by Tetragon, London
Printed and bound by TJ Books, Padstow, Cornwall

This work is supported by the Anglo-Swedish Literary Foundation.

The authorised representative in the EU for product safety and
compliance is Easy Access System Europe – Mustamäe tee 50,
10621 Tallinn, Estonia, gpsr.requests@easproject.com

AGNES LIDBECK is one of Sweden's most prominent and versatile contemporary writers. She made her literary debut with *Supporting Act* in 2017, which was shortlisted for the Svenska Dagbladet Prize and won the Borås Tidning Debut Novel Prize. She went on to write *Förlåten* ('Forgiven', 2018), *Gå förlorad* ('Get Lost', 2019), *Nikes bok* ('Nike's Book', 2021) and *All min kärlek* ('All my Love', 2023). Lidbeck also writes for the stage and is known for her sharp, minimalist style.

NICHOLA SMALLEY is a translator of Swedish and Norwegian literature. Her translation of Andrzej Tichý's *Wretchedness* won the 2021 Oxford-Weidenfeld Prize and was shortlisted for the Bernard Shaw and International Booker Prizes. Her translation of *A System So Magnificent It Is Blinding* by Amanda Svensson was longlisted for the International Booker Prize 2023.

SUPPORTING
ACT

For Karin

The social contract is not negotiated at an individual level. It is universal, a set of rules that must be followed in order for society to function.

The fundamental requirement is that a woman play three roles. She must be a mother. She must be desirable. She must provide care.

Each role must be played in accordance with agreed guidelines. Her responses are predetermined. Improvisation is reserved for those of unsound mind.

It is the woman who has the most to gain from maintaining these boundaries. As long as she remains comprehensible to those around her, she will also be comprehensible to herself.

The opposite, being incomprehensible, is something she must fear: a symptom of a physiological or empathic shortcoming.

PART ONE

An event becomes relevant only once it has consequences.

For that reason, the story begins at the moment the woman becomes a mother.

Before that, it was a children's fairy tale, without the restrictions of logic, with surreal elements and many possible endings.

The room to which Anna and Jens are moved after the birth has three high windows. It is quiet, and outside the sun is shining. Anna sits up in the bed and holds her first, naked child to her naked breast. It is recommended: it stimulates bonding and milk production.

Jens sits alongside with his finger, the very tip, in the child's hand. Jens is drinking cordial and eating cheese sandwiches from a tray bearing the Swedish flag, which they knew would be there, which they'd joked about beforehand. A Swedish flag, how vulgar. Christ, they said in unison once the midwife had left. Anna is drinking coffee.

Over the next twenty-four hours, the midwives come by roughly every other hour, different women, all pausing at the door. Sometimes Anna calls for them with a red button to check that everything is as it should be, that new twitches in the child's eyelids and changes in its temperature and the shooting pains down her side are as they should be.

During these visits, Anna looks at the midwives, who look at the bag of urine hanging from between Anna's legs and at the few thick beads of milk she manages to press out of her nipples. She feels them palpate her abdomen and she sees them looking at the blood collected in her sanitary pad. She sees them handing her pills, she sees them weighing her child.

Anna wants to give the child all the names she has ever heard. It is covered in a layer of white wax. On its head is a blood-flecked cotton cap. It opens its bright eyes and looks at Anna and she looks back. Then the child parts its lips and begins to scream.

Anna sleeps poorly at night. She doesn't have enough milk. The child is yellow and hot and she can feel it shrinking away in her hands. Soon it will lie completely cold like a squirrel in a box, she thinks, an image from her childhood. It lies there, jutting its chin against her breast but unable to latch on. She calls for the midwives again and again but they've seen this before. They refuse to panic.

Their calm rubs off on Jens. He feeds the child with a little spoon, drop by drop. His patience is boundless, but sometimes when the child is sleeping he leaves the room. Anna can't understand how that is possible, how he can absent himself. Jens showers and changes his clothes at home and comes back with things she needs, that she has sent him home to fetch, but also with a clean scent around him, fresh air. The blood between Anna's legs smells of salt.

Anna walks through the hospital corridor with the child in a transparent trolley. It's important to get the circulation going as soon as possible after a caesarean. There are other people in the corridor, mostly new fathers gone to get drinks or sandwiches.

Anna wonders whether the fathers want her, or would want her, or will want her later. She wonders if they can look past her current unflattering circumstances and see that she ordinarily moves in a different way, that she normally wears her hair differently. Then the child wails and she returns to her room.

On the third day, her breasts tighten and ache and the milk starts to flow. They are allowed to go home then, and they are allowed to take the child with them. Jens drives the car. Anna sits in the back seat and closes her eyes, fearful of a sudden accident. The child is a boy. Harry, after Anna's father. Jens says, Of course, darling.

Jens changes nappies full of black meconium: the hair the child has swallowed in the womb, he tells Anna, though she was the one who gave him the book that said all that. When he talks to the child his voice is different to how it is with Anna or on the telephone.

They give Harry vitamins and formula milk, a supplement. Jens holds the spoon. Anna sits on the sofa with the pump whirring at her breast. This way Jens can do every other feed and develop a bond, and she gets to sleep too, in theory.

Anna has to strain to maintain a rational relationship to the milk machine and the blue rubber ring around her nipple, just as she has to strain to maintain a level of equanimity in her relationship with Jens, who, far from realizing that the situation is humiliating, stares at her and asks, Where's the extra pack of nappies, darling? Getting angry with him would be childish, Anna thinks. Only naive people fail to understand that children change everything. It would be pointless to become overwhelmed.

*

It would be naive to become overwhelmed. The instruction books have warned Anna that she will experience emotional changes. Becoming a mother is the biggest thing that will happen in your life, they said, and Anna waits obediently for this biggest thing to take its toll.

The bond is another thing she has read about. And indeed, Anna does experience a gradually increasing sense of responsibility for Harry, one she interprets as love. It's a relief to feel her body reacting in accordance with the diagrams.

After about five days, which is a little late perhaps but not a catastrophe, he feels like a genuine part of her life: no longer so absurd, though still fragile. Anna sees Harry's pulse beating in his fontanelle and wonders whether that's normal or if it means he'll soon die. She rings the doctor for advice. Jens scans the books. Anna puts a cap on Harry so she doesn't have to see the pulsating skin.

While the bond makes everyday life easier, it leaves her feeling disappointed. The hormone and salt levels in her blood never give her the intense emotions she's read they should. She's been led to believe that the sense of unity will feel sacrosanct, that it will be an excuse for impulses, that she will begin to act like a lion without feeling foolish. But the child doesn't make her forget herself, being a mother doesn't shut out all other thoughts. She's very aware that many of the details of motherhood are ridiculous, like parodies or bad art. She blushes when she catches herself sniffing Harry's head.

She sees herself studying his nostrils and listening to his breathing without being able to forget herself. She thinks:

isn't it bizarre, I'm admiring his smooth elbows and I'm dying for him to grab my finger!

For Anna's body, the pregnancy has had far-reaching consequences. The iron in her blood is almost gone. Her skeleton has shifted. She preferred the old centres of gravity. The birth made these consequences worse and added new ones. At the clinic they rub a blue salve on the scar on her abdomen. The skin around it is numb. She scrapes off the glue left by the plasters. The lines they drew to mark the sites for the anaesthesia and incision take a surprisingly long time to fade.

The mucous membranes in her genitals and her throat have dried out. The discharge comes and goes. Sometimes it is pale red, sometimes dark red, sometimes almost yellow. She rolls the pads in paper and puts them in the bin. She empties the bins regularly but still thinks the apartment smells of blood.

The pain moves around. Sometimes it is in the small of her back, sometimes in her neck. She gets haemorrhoids that itch and sting but can't stop herself from touching them, trying to push them back into her rectum. She is constipated, she drinks a lot of water. My sweat smells of bread, she thinks.

Anna calls the child *Harry* or *he* when she talks about him. He is her most common topic of conversation.

Anna obeys Harry's will. She makes the excuse to others that his routine, his temperament or his desire for this or that guides her. She spends her days in anticipation of his needing her again. She sits in a chair while he sleeps, waiting for him to awaken.

Anna bathes Harry in lukewarm water and dips her elbow to check it is the right temperature. When the light falls in a certain way through the window and she lifts him high over her head or makes some other graceful movement, she imagines someone can see her. Often it is one of the men before Jens. She imagines that they are standing along the walls and that they see her in this intimacy with the child and that they are jealous of the child.

She lowers her arms into the water as he rests in her hands; she thinks there is a special sheen to her hair as she lays Harry against her shoulder and walks around over the warm, sun-dappled parquet. She imagines the men following her from room to room.

The mother's rules of conduct are simple. This is a necessity, since the mother has not slept and has difficulty following more complex instructions.

The mother must not become hungry. She must produce food. The mother must not moan. She must bear. The mother must hum predetermined, archaic melodies.

She must also be able to perform some of these melodies on the piano, with one or two fingers.

Six months pass. Anna's days follow a regular schedule of shower and haircare in the morning, a pre-lunch walk and black coffee in a paper cup, picking at salad and gossiping with one friend or another while they each attempt to ascertain whose arms, breasts and stomach have grown the most since pregnancy; who shows the most presence in the moment, who shows a longing to return to sensible conversation, and who shows how sick she is of wiping away vomit; who thought the lunch important enough for eyeshadow, and who is too busy for that. Who dresses their child in pale blue and pink and who dresses it in grey and yellow.

The stretch marks across her breasts, abdomen and thighs fade but still lie like a net over her skin. The scar from the birth, a surgical procedure, fades too but lingers in the lightest of shades as a reminder. After showering, Anna fingers her stomach. It still hasn't regained full sensation. She thinks about how she has been opened, lain exposed, how someone has held her intestines in their hands.

*

Anna is precise with Harry's food and his baths, his nappy changes and his clothing. She sets the egg timer and makes sure he gets his fifteen minutes a day on his front, his fifteen minutes of story time. She takes him out to get some fresh air every day.

Harry accepts her, as one does who is given everything. Sometimes he cries. Not because of negligence, she tells herself, but rather as a temporary symptom of hunger or cold or something else she has the power to remedy as soon as they've made it home from their walk.

Anna sleeps in short bursts with her arms around Harry, who she places on top of her to avoid crushing or smothering him or one of those other things she has read mothers do when they are tired. When she wakes her elbows ache, they are stiff. When she sits, she rocks from side to side. When she stands, she rocks from foot to foot.

Anna moves about silently. She often kneels in front of Harry. When he lies on the floor she sits with her legs spread wide. If she is sitting in a chair, he digs his hands into her. Harry gets his first tooth. Anna feels it scrape against her nipple.

Harry continues to leave his marks on her. They have the effect of making the present and the past flow together. She recalls sexual encounters from the time before parenthood. Her nipples become drawn out, red and painful. Bruises bloom on the insides of her arms. He vomits white liquid on her shoulders, stomach and hastily pulled-up underwear.

Harry's voice, his feet in her hands, his need for her, responses she cannot control, manifestations from within her body. In this way, this antithesis to sex resembles nothing so much as porn. Anna's glands answer to Harry, her focus is entirely on him. And still this is meant to be emotionally distinct, fundamentally separate from her reactions to a man. All those times I played the slave, Anna thinks, and to think I got it so right.

(A slave is more ridiculous in reality than in theory. It's a woman on her knees, wiping something up without paying attention to the curve of her back. Life as a slave is wonderful when you believe you are playing the submissive. Subservience can be charged with all sorts of thrills until your knees start to hurt and the game doesn't stop.)

Anna sits on the bed and Harry sleeps between her thighs with his feet against her crotch. He sleeps across her knees, he sucks on her knuckles. The fumbling hands grasping at her throat have a different meaning than masculine hands that once carried out the same movements. She sees her throat in the mirror and wonders what she should liken it to now.

There is a place there, halfway up towards the ear on her left side, that she used to give to men and tell them it was a spot no one else would have access to: a gesture of exclusivity. Now Harry grinds his hairless head against it, and against everything else. There are no millimetres left to grant anyone sole rights to, Anna thinks, wondering if she is sacrificing herself enough when she gives her all.

When Harry is looked after by Jens's mother, Anna's heart is in her mouth; there's a sour taste. When he allows himself to be picked up by other female relatives, that same heart beats very hard. She sees his hands in their hair and knows she is replaceable.

Harry is the individual, the centre, Anna thinks. I am here for him but if I die now he'll not remember me, she thinks. If I walked out, everyone would remember it, she thinks, and also: If he died, everyone would remember me.

The thought of Harry's death makes her palms tingle. So she says to Harry's grandmother that he mustn't eat grapes and thinks that she is the only one who really cares about him not choking, that it is still only she who is the mother. She rings the medical hotline to enquire about his rashes, his snot.

Anna bites off Harry's soft nails with her teeth instead of cutting them with scissors. She follows his fingertips; they are still completely smooth against her tongue. She massages him with oil, scentless oil. She massages between his toes and the creases of his arms.

Anna hushes soothingly and wipes up first her own milk, then baby food, then cordial that has splashed from the straw. Anna wipes the table clean of lumps of soggy biscuit. Anna mixes cordial and salt to make a fluid replacement when Harry has been sick, and she gives him the fluid from a teaspoon until he is sick again. She takes off the pillowcase and wipes the sick from his nose and ears.

Anna does these things again and again. She also does a thousand other things, automatically, as though her bone marrow had prior knowledge.

When Anna became pregnant, Jens and Anna said they were expecting, *they* were expecting in plural. Down to the detail, Anna's eating habits, drinking habits and the height of her heels were their common concern. Her sleeping patterns and her backache were their sleeping patterns and their backache. She heard Jens talk about her body with his mother on the phone. He had the phone clamped between his shoulder and his ear; she saw him at an angle from behind.

Now it is not her body he's talking about but Harry's. The telephone is still clamped between his shoulder and his ear. With his hand he rocks Harry's bouncer instead of stroking Anna's sore back, or he holds up his palm to protect himself while Harry thumps him with a wooden train.

Jens mirrors Harry's expressions, grimacing as he discusses the child's height and weight and hair, his stomach and his pincer grip.

There's nothing abstract about Harry's growth, it can be put into words. He is literally growing out of Anna's hands. He gets longer than Jens's forearm, heavier than a shopping bag. He headbutts Anna's chin. Jens and Anna talk about how early he is learning to sit up, crawl and stand compared to other people's children.

Anna meets Harry's gaze and breaks into a grin, saying, Cuc-koo. All the while she is calculating how long it is since Jens slept with her, not counting his business trips.

I must not show dissatisfaction, Anna thinks, I must not show my rage. What rage, Anna asks herself, what do I have to feel rage about?

Anna sits on the metro and sees the men getting on and off. She flicks through their faces and wonders if they want her, or would want her, or will want her later, when she is wearing clothes that are not intended for the park. Then Harry cries in his buggy and Anna gets out the dummy. She puts away her thoughts of men, folding up their faces and stuffing them into her handbag for another time. There is no time now in any case, no room in any case.

When she is alone at home, Anna cannot bring herself to talk to Harry, even though you are supposed to talk to children to help with bonding and language development. She blames it on tiredness or maybe hormones and starts taking iron tablets, magnesium and echinacea to stop her nails splitting and to give her the energy to sing.

Her nails grow stronger. Harry lies on the changing table and looks at Anna and Anna changes his nappies with a practised hand. She does not find them disgusting, but she damn well hasn't got the energy to sing 'The Wheels on the Bus', not even one more time. Not 'Three Blind Mice' either.

Harry spends more and more time awake. He used to follow Anna with his gaze, now he follows on his knees, now on his rounded feet. March comes and she puts him in his chair in the sun and he waves his arms and makes noises. July comes and she puts him in his buggy in the shade and in his bed without a cover, she gives him wooden spoons to bang, bells to ring, soft mirrors that look like little lakes. He starts to cry anyway, or makes other noises that Anna guesses she ought to respond to.

If only there were other people about, I could look after him without— she interrupts the thought before it gets to the words *boredom, anxiety, rage*. Then I'd be able to say *oo oo oo, do do do, ma-ma ma-ma ma-ma* and *toowit-toowoo* so someone would hear it and see how much I'm giving, the shape of my lips when I give it.

So she starts going out.

Anna goes along to baby singing and baby swimming and playgroup. She goes to mother and baby groups and the church's baby club and parent and baby cinema screenings. She goes to baby massage and tries going to a centre where you meet immigrant women to talk to about their babies. It helps a little, thanks to or perhaps in spite of the fact that the room is full of other mothers talking to one another while bouncing their babies casually on their knees, like she is doing.

Anna sits in a circle on the floor of the church hall with the others. The carpet is blue and Harry is trying to wriggle out of her arms, away from her knees, over to the basket of rattles. Anna smiles apologetically and wonders whether it seems like Harry is confident or whether it seems like he does not like her.

Harry's mamma is how she introduces herself when her turn comes. Oh yeah, sorry, my name's Anna, she adds with a feeble half-laugh. She heard another mother do the same in a different circle the previous week. Anna thought it seemed a bit special. To get so little sleep, so little you forget your own name but never the child's.

The mother must signal her role, as well as her socio-economic group, through appropriate accessories.

For example, she may carry a tote bag in her hand rather than a leather bag over her shoulder. Further options include preferring coffee without milk, a rounder watch, or a lower heel.

As an extension of these external attributes, the mother must express the emotions the observer associates with the role. It is desirable, but not a requirement, that she also feel the emotions she embodies.

The mother must make a house a home. She must choose colours for the walls. The mother must determine which kind of bread is to be eaten in this family, if we eat bread in this family.

The decisions that must be made are numerous, the tasks that must be undertaken equally so. The functional duties may be drawn out over time, to conceal the gaps between them.

A mother must wipe the mirror clean of toothpaste flecks, ensure the sink is free from saliva and wipe the toilet seat clean of urine. In addition, a mother must place flowers in vases and smile in surprise at drawings in red and green.

Anna stands in the kitchen, heating water for baby rice, for things Harry can eat without choking. From the kitchen, Anna sees Jens turning into a father. She can see his gaze shifting focus. It shows in his pupils, in the distance they fix upon. She can see it in the wrinkles around his eyes, the way they become more pronounced when he smiles at the child and throws it up towards the ceiling.

Jens goes to work in the morning. In the evening he comes home and goes straight over to Harry and picks him up if he is playing on the floor, or takes him from Anna's arms if she has picked him up because something has happened and he needs soothing. Jens bathes Harry and talks to him. He plays his records for Harry, like he did for Anna when they first met.

Anna stands in the kitchen, boiling vegetables until they are just soft enough. From the kitchen, Anna hears Jens turning into a father. Jens sings nursery rhymes, he sings songs. He sings Bowie for Harry. He plays his guitar and dances with Harry to Leonard Cohen, slowly he waltzes Harry to the music. He reads to Harry and points at the pictures on the walls: See that, Harry? Do you think it might be a bird?

Jens talks to Harry: We'll be playing chess soon. He tells him about the boat, in official terminology. Soon we'll be skating, he says. He asks Harry if he likes Genesis. Gaga, Harry says.

Previously, Anna put on clothes that would make Jens want to take them off her so she would get to say no so he could turn it into a yes. But she cannot be dealing in such subtleties now. There is neither the time nor the energy for suggestion, other than in their muted rows.

Many years later, in relationship counselling, Jens explains that he felt uncomfortable with the idea of mixing sexuality and small children, that he thought everything has its time, that there are cycles in life, but that sex felt like such a clear expectation. A demand for normative masculinity, the therapist will suggest, helping him formulate his words, and Jens will nod in agreement.

Anna will be surprised and take it as a criticism, as though she were normative. She will use the word *hurt* about his having felt that way. As far as she is concerned, she doesn't have the tools to insist.

Even then, Anna will not be able to put this feeling into words. Despite the time that has passed, she still will not have the capacity to say that she has never seen it as her job to initiate intercourse – what value would it have then? That she only felt at ease with being persuaded, being resistant, being overcome.

She will say she did not want to nag, but she will not be able to say she wanted to refuse. The things it is not possible to find words for now will not be possible to find

32

words for then either: the body, the power of the body, the power of refusal, the power to refuse.

But the years have not yet passed. Now it is now: now it is Friday evening. Harry pulls a tube of toothpaste across the floor while Anna shaves her legs and washes her hair.

Because she cannot be the one to decide when intercourse is to take place, her skin must always be ready. Particularly on Fridays and Saturdays, when they drink wine. There is a tradition. When she is hairless and dry, she anoints her skin so she will be moist again.

Up! Harry says.

When intercourse does take place, it is in reaction to some stimulus Anna is not aware of or does not feel she has a part in.

On occasion Jens turns to her when they are about to go to sleep, and he touches her. Anna is unsure. Why is he doing this now, she thinks, why not another time? We've neither argued nor made up, there's no motive. Is it simply something in his body that needs to be channelled, or has he slept with someone else, is that why he wants to sleep with me now?

She does not ask. She takes a constructive approach. Anna licks her fingers discreetly to aid penetration. She cannot cry out, cannot resist, because that would wake the child. So there is nothing to feel, no texture. She is not overcome, she is not overpowered, she is just there as a practicality. They already know each other, so what should she do with her hands? What is the point without a struggle? Anna wonders, and yet still she feels relieved that he wants to.

Awkward, dissolute. It's no particular will that makes him empty himself into me, Anna thinks. It's not a test of strength. Not proof that he loves me in particular. I am simply accessible, I am the closest thing.

When Jens has come, he falls asleep. Later Harry wakes and she gives him a bottle so he will fall asleep again. She sits on the edge of the bed and waits until he has sucked it down. She listens to the rain falling on the roof. Winters pass, Christmas rolls around again, then spring. The apartment starts to fill up. The walls are no longer so white, the floors feel filthy from dropped fruit.

It is not as fun to put tulips in a vase when there are crayons and dusty stickers and toy soldiers under the table, but however much Anna bends down and tidies them away there is always something there.

Goddamn fucking motherfucking balls, darling, Jens swears as he creeps in through the darkness after a delayed flight back from Oslo and steps on Lego. Jens gets Anna pregnant again, a mixture of will and forgetfulness and expectation. If they're going to move they should do it now, before Harry starts school. Before he's built a network, darling, as Jens puts it. Anna packs boxes. Her stomach is in the way. She packs her clothes and she packs her cookbooks and she packs her children, the one who is at nursery school and the one who is kicking her in the ribs. She squats in the basement corridor and tugs at boxes.

Harry is almost four when Hedda is born. Hedda lies on a scarf and follows Anna with her gaze, yet another gaze.

When Anna takes a break – when she has slammed the cookbook shut and wiped the stove, when the tasting spoon has been leant against the side of the pot and she has dried her hands on the stiffly pressed hand towel – she leans over Hedda and makes the faces one makes.

Hedda's gaze is not enough of an answer. Anna imagines instead that one of her neighbours can see her, one of the tall men who do the same things as Jens in the garden but remain unfamiliar. She takes Hedda to the office with her, she lets the people there see the child sleeping in the buggy. She gives glimpses, through loose clothing, of how narrow her own waist is again. She orders photographs to be framed, photographs of the family against a white background.

When a woman becomes a mother, the unit of measurement for her worth shifts from that denoting her power to attract to that denoting her body's durability.

Motherhood can be likened to the wearing of religiously coded clothing. The flesh becomes anonymous, suited for things other than desire.

The mother must not be an individual who – through the force of her unique proportions, waistline to nail length – can be distinguished from others.

For that reason, she must no longer be called by a name or by some onomatopoeic metaphor. Instead, she must, like all tools, be named for her function.

While Anna lives through the practical caregiving that is her life, and the years pass, she toys with the thought of what will follow, of what she will do with her time when it is returned to her. She imagines a series of actions she will have the opportunity to undertake then, and how she will be as a person when her days are no longer spent wiping things up.

The thought is a dangerous game; playing with an afterwards frightens her. The first time Hedda pours herself a glass of milk without spilling any, Anna's mouth fills with the salty taste of blood. The reduced dependency of her children is like a door left ajar. Beyond it waits a void that may be emptiness or may be space.

Anna hides the birthday flag in a special place, she tells a story only she can tell with a voice only she can speak in, and she collects jars to fill with berries that only she can find. Anna picks blackberries. There are black stains. The branches catch at her arms. The flies circle. She remembers names no one else remembers. All this, she thinks, will be meaningful in the long term too. They would miss my jam, she thinks; Christmas isn't Christmas without the angel chimes.

Between the traditions, more years pass and she eats different types of grains in her salad and she notes which of her friends let their hair go grey and which of them are still wearing jeans that are much too tight and which have their children attend more than five activities and which let them take the bus alone and whose babysitter speaks English and whose children still get given raisins instead of sweets on a Saturday.

On the basis of all this information, she tries to establish some kind of identity. It is possible to define, somewhere in there, what she does, how she is, what she prefers. Who she is.

Anna scribbles numbers on the back of an envelope as she talks on the phone. The numbers turn into flowers, the flowers get coloured in black, the black shapes become squares, she throws the envelope in the wastepaper basket.

If he beat me I could leave, Anna thinks, and she means Jens and a different type of beating from the one she dreams of, the kind you must not accept. But he never beats me, that's the problem.

If he drank I could leave, she thinks, but he doesn't, not enough. If he were seeing someone else I could leave, in anger, or if he told enough lies. But the easiest thing would be if he died.

Every time Jens comes home late from work, from his trips, or late back from something else, she moves restlessly from room to room. Is this the night it will happen? The streets are icy. Which dress would I wear to the funeral? Maybe, if he is tired enough, a cat, a deer, a careless turn.

No veil. Just dark circles under my eyes. My sorrow, Anna thinks, that's how deep it would be.

But Jens does not die, he does not start drinking, he does not beat her. Regardless of how bad the weather is, she hears the door open sooner or later, and he comes in, suggests a cup of tea, suggests some TV, holds her feet as they sit on the sofa, remembers names and conversations and asks about work and takes her side and agrees that the situation is terrible, agrees on Italy this year rather than France and agrees that it has been a long time since we saw them and agrees that it is time to prune the apple tree and stands on the ladder and saws off the branches and doesn't saw himself, even though she can see how the saw might slip, and drives the cuttings to the tip and comes home and barbecues lamb and pours wine and strokes hair. A stubborn refusal to set her free, to leave her, to let her have something to resent him for.

And yet the way he sits on the sofa, Anna thinks, is a reason to detest. Arms spread wide across the back. Wider than the width of his shoulders and the length of his arms requires him to. An aerial photo would show the way he spreads himself out, Anna thinks, and she sits still, with her feet on his lap.

Anna has a large collection of rings and bracelets. With several of them on at the same time there is a clinking, jingling noise. She had the ones she'd inherited from her grandma and mother to begin with, then Jens noticed how much joy she got from jewellery, so now she gets new bracelets and rings in velvet boxes every Christmas and every birthday and how exciting is that?

Anna gives the trinkets to Hedda to play with. The chains get tangled. Anna shouts at Hedda: Do you have to destroy everything of mine? Or that's what she shouts in her head; what comes out, pressed tight through her lips, is a sigh.

Summer rolls around, summer rolls around, summer rolls around a third, fourth, seventh time in a row. Time no longer registers. No one can know how many lilos have been blown up, how many have faded from memory. Hedda wants to be spun round, in the water or to music. Her hands in Anna's and her arms straight out in front. And of course Anna spins, eternally, she spins Hedda through the air.

Hedda becomes a wave formation, she rises and falls until Anna can no longer go on. No longer be grinning, spinning. Until her arms are tired and it is her head that is spinning. But Hedda never tires, is never satisfied, never says *Thank you, Mamma*, just pesters for more: *Spin me, Mamma! Spin me!*

All Anna's joy at spinning her daughter – so free, with her head back and the sleeves of her shirt pushed carelessly up to her elbows – suddenly vanishes when it is still not enough, when she is never done spinning.

However much Anna grits her teeth and does jigsaws or listens to what the children say, it is never enough. However happy she appears, there will be another hour or another day when she must be happy again.

The strain is too much. Her patience runs out before the game is over and the heat she feels in her throat then, the heat from their ungrateful arguments, almost tips into rage, would certainly have done so were it not for the fact that she never gets angry.

Anna clatters the jigsaw pieces together or turns off the music and then there is always something: cushions on the floor or towels on the floor or ketchup on the cushions or a toy soldier who needs fixing and pieces that do not fit; something that means that she, with severe movements and a severe voice, has to say, *Heavens, we can't have it looking like this, heavens, we can't live in a pigsty, you know, will you never learn to tidy your things away, I'm not your cleaner.*

And so she is always the one who is like that: stumblingly close to angry, instead of being the happy one. The angry one is someone no one wants to see.

The children run to Jens in the other room or out onto the lawn. With him they find a dead bird to bury, the neighbour's cat must have caught it. She hears Jens making a big number of it: Fetch me the box, fetch me the spade, don't touch. They disappear under the apple tree in their raincoats and they come back a little later, all full of something and with earth on their fingers and they say to her, Look at my cross, Mamma, look at my wreath, Mamma, sing a song about God, Mamma, and Anna grits her teeth and says, I'm in the middle of making lunch, I really don't have time.

Anna works on life as though it can be got in order. She buys new wet-weather gear for the children with a vague idea that such an action might be final. They wear out the elastic straps underfoot – at first they get wet and full of gravel, then they break. It drives me mad that you can never take care of your things, Anna says to the children. Heavens, put your hat in the drawer, she says.

Anna goes to work only to go home, Anna goes home only to make pancakes, Anna makes pancakes only for them to get eaten. Anna says, I haven't stood here making pancakes only for you not to eat.

Hedda's movements – she is the younger one, the more childlike – are a reminder, a mockery. She plays with stones, sticks and other junk she has picked up on the way home from nursery school. Her games are drawn-out. She claims to be the only one with her forename in the whole world, as though she were the only one of her kind.

Anna rolls her shoulders and climbs up on a stool to reach the mixer unit Jens insists on putting on the highest shelf. Mamma! the children shout. They are a choir of two, in counterpoint.

Anna climbs down from the stool without having reached the mixer. She goes into the living room. You never know, they might have done themselves serious harm. She can't look for the mixer if they have cut themselves on glass, if a window has been smashed, if one of them has fallen through the window and smashed their skull in.

When Harry is seven, Anna buys vegetarian cookbooks, when he is nine, an unusual rosebush: the rose takes and flowers, they eat delicious meals with a lot of pine nuts, but still nothing has changed.

Anna selects sweaters according to the weather. She clears withered flowers from the table if they are no longer beautiful, but not before that; they are allowed to drop petals on the tabletop.

Anna can afford to have short hair, she buys shoes that need taking care of, she can afford not to take care of them. Anna starts giving monthly donations to the Red Cross, takes out a membership for the concert hall, finds a piano teacher for the children. The garden plants find their way into the house, in small still lifes in which the colours are absolutely right for each other.

To get through one day is to undertake every aspect of it in the right order and in a correct manner. It requires her to undertake her tasks, whatever these are, without breaking into that voice, the one that makes it known that something unsuitable has occurred.

There are days that are difficult to get through. Days when she goes about with an itch in her nostrils. Her breathing and pulse become faster. She feels her fingers swell, her rings become tighter, the grease seeping from the follicles in her scalp. Coffee tastes burnt, even when drunk from her new cup. She sees sudden images of things that have happened and blushes despite the many years that have passed. Walk out or have it out, her heart hammers. As though either were an option.

In the end she does neither. The day passes. The neighbours can see into the garden. There is nowhere to hide in the house either; none of the doors can be locked any more, not even those to the bathroom and the toilets. She is the one who has removed all the locks, at the thought that someone might drown, the thought that someone might go and lock themselves in a room and that in the room terrible things would happen. Perhaps the children would be there together and inflict some awful harm on one another. Perhaps one of them would be in there alone, with the water running, and bang their head and drown in a centimetre of water.

Perhaps something else might happen, something no one would have had a reason to worry about until the child opened the bathroom door and it had already happened.

She remembers the story of the mother who died in the bathroom when she slipped, about to bathe her child. The father came home and found her dead and the child sitting in the bath splashing. If that happened, it would still be the right choice, to be the one who had died. She always had to listen out for the children when they were small.

Their shrieking was a reassurance, it meant they had not yet died. That all her daydreams of them being dead and of her being free and sorrowful and interesting had not been realized. That's no way to think.

The mother can never be high-minded or magnanimous. All her efforts must be made as a matter of course. Not even when her children are scratching her eyes out and she does not scratch theirs out in return, is it any more than that which is expected.

The mother can be irritated by milk stains or clumps of dust. Never by the children themselves. A child may be berated for taking up all the space on the sofa, but not for taking up all the space in one's life.

The mother must raise her children to hang up their jackets. The mother may become a little tired when they forget to hang up their jackets.

She must not say anything when they wake at night from dreams they cannot put into words and when they try to get into her bed to put their feet between her thighs.

Neither can she say anything about the older child no longer keeping her warm in this way.

Things – crumbs, piles of washing, bits of tape – may be given as the causes of a mother's frustration.

Sometimes the right word comes out but with the wrong tone, which is almost as dangerous as the wrong word. Perhaps it depends on the weather, Anna thinks. She feels pressure in her forehead; it could be an incoming low-pressure system or a tumour.

The children will never sit properly on their chairs by themselves, she has to push them in hard. They scrape their cutlery, she is forced to hear it. The alternative to their scraping cutlery would be her yelling out loud so someone would hear her.

Afterwards, after she has almost screamed, her hands start to itch and a film of cold sweat coats her palms. She wants to fall to her knees before the children and beg their forgiveness for having heard the panic in her voice, or whatever it was: not rage, just this endless rain, the third day in a row now, a life.

If I could only escape, she thinks, just get away for a while, the noise in my head would stop and I would be able to catch hold of it, that kite, and never let it crash again into the middle of the children's picnic, crashing down so the cords cut their cheeks. She thinks of herself as a dancing kite, carried by the wind – never away, but always flung downwards; she thinks she is a danger to the thing holding her in place.

Don't show your rage, thinks Anna as she wraps the cheese in cling film, except through your lack of appetite, she thinks, pushing her plate away; no more than a cat flicks its tail, she thinks, her face towards the refrigerator; no more than a stylized claw as a substitute for real violence, she thinks, closing the door silently on the sleepers.

Anna has officially had one abortion. It is registered in her story about herself, an official wound to grieve. It was so long ago now that she cannot summon any emotional reaction to it, but it still makes her uncontradictable in certain kinds of anecdotal discussions of women's rights.

It would, however, be impossible to have more than one abortion and maintain one's credibility. One abortion can be bad luck, something to battle one's conscience about. One day to remember each year, to count the years from. More than that is seen as sloppy. You cannot suffer from something you have done multiple times.

That is why she hides the abortion she has when Harry is eight and Hedda is four, hides it from Jens and also from herself. It passes unremarked, less than a manicure, less than a new juicer in both scope and cost.

Thursday comes around, eleven at night, a body full of exhaustion, a head that cannot stop associating. Too much screen time, thinks Anna, and pictures laundry on a line strung between two trees. White laundry in the breeze. An attempt to calm her thoughts. Her chest heaves, tears fill her eyes. She wishes the children were sick. She wishes they were little and sick and had woken up, so she could console them about something.

Lying beside the person you know so well and still trying to creep imperceptibly closer: as though rejection would be less painful if it were not spoken out loud.

She curves her back but still Jens does not press himself against her. She breathes as though she is sleeping and he soon drifts off. She lies awake, tense so as to be as clear as possible: here are my arse and thighs, there is no belly here, here are my breasts, where a hand might land as if by accident. Jens will not wake; she feels her construction crumble: her arse and thighs suddenly insignificant, her stomach bearing the traces of two children, her breasts too, they are used up and have no further meaning. What gives him the right to respond or not respond as he wants? What is this mechanism that gives him this right to have other thoughts in his head?

Everything Anna has read tells her that men get eaten up inside if they do not get it. *It*; she avoids the word *sex* even in her thoughts, but it is *sex* she means by *it*. She avoids the words *whore*, *cunt*, she thinks of folding soft sweaters but the thought returns, the thought is back in her body and her body is measured in those terms, the ones that must not be used.

She thinks, cannot stop herself thinking, that her form of power is being able to permit or not permit him to touch

49

her. But he doesn't want to touch her and so she has no power. I have no power, Anna thinks. I cannot withhold a thing he does not want.

She never wonders where she might direct him. The thought always stops there: at the scene where he wants and she does not. Where she has something and he reaches out his hands. That is where she has to turn away.

Summer comes, it rains, it has been raining for weeks now, or perhaps just since yesterday. Anna makes a second cup of coffee, mostly to pass the time. She makes some dough, to pass the time. She invents small tasks for the children: put the Lego in the box, do a drawing for Daddy, help me pour out the sunflower seeds. Still the time does not pass.

Hedda practises skipping on the kitchen floor. She can't get the rope going, she doesn't have the strength. Her feet hit the floor without rhythm. She swings the rope over her head, steps over it, all the while singing a song. *What shall we do with the drunken sailor?* she sings tunelessly, loudly. Sometimes she says *Look at me, Mamma.*

It continues raining. Anna irons the washing. Harry sits on the floor alongside the ironing board, or rather he leans back, pushing himself round with his feet. Aimlessly, ants in his pants, he wants to play on the computer but is not allowed; no way is he going out. Anna has not decided whether to start nagging.

The time will not pass. The time must be broken down into small sections, as with colouring in. One square at a time: the pouring of yogurt into the breakfast bowls square, the reminder to eat yogurt square. The clear the table square, the sweep under the table square. The check teeth-brushing and the brush hair squares. In the evening Jens watches TV with the children, she hears him getting involved, hears them laughing at something.

The mother's relationship to the child is linear. It wanes as the child outgrows its childhood. In the moment, the passage of time is abstract. But on a wall it can be marked in centimetres.

The child's liberation is gradual, as the inevitable often is. It doesn't let go of the mother's hand with a sudden gesture, as at the end of a sexual relationship: Don't ever touch me again! First it spits out the breast. Then it is devoured by the world.

It should not be interpreted as a sign of infidelity when the child stops clinging to the mother's kneecap for balance, stops stroking her cheek with its nails, stops calling out Mamma! at night.

So there is no reasonable cause for the mother to distance herself to an equivalent degree. She must not lose interest in tickling the child's neck. Tickling the child's neck remains a minimum requirement.

The child's periodic returns must be welcomed. When it once again wishes to touch the mother, she must feel gratitude.

Anna tidies the house. She reorganizes the hallway, the basement, the attic: the places where remnants gather.

It's mostly Jens's things: objects whose use is opaque to her still, their expectations of her unfamiliar. His vinyl collection, boathooks, and other things that are part of the compromise, that are the compromise in concrete form. In the summer we sail.

Her teeth are chipped; Anna runs her tongue over them. She never shows her teeth when smiling, she has assumed a calm expression, the big smile disappearing somewhere along with the little rage. In the mornings when she wakes, she has to press the muscles beneath her ears with her thumb to release the tension enough for her to be able to swallow or do anything more than smile, a little, with her lips together.

Anna lies in bed with her back a taut bow and reads her book and tries to look like a cat, something Jens might like to stroke, but still with claws. She lies there, expectant, and after a while she hears his breathing change; it grows heavier and she thinks something is going to happen soon.

She is careful not to look over. She is careful to turn the page with an indolent paw. When several seconds have passed she hears the breaths grow even deeper. Jens has fallen asleep on his back. Again. She remembers the scene from before: another book, a cooler evening, all those cool evenings with the street lamp through the window.

Anna swallows the saliva that is a sign of rage. I cannot show the rage now, that would be weakness, that would be wanting something. I am not angry, Anna thinks. She thinks of white laundry, hung between trees. She breathes.

Roughly once every six months she thinks she will talk to Jens. She thinks she will say: What you needed from me, you no longer need. Or else she might say: What you needed from me, you no longer want. *You no longer need* is probably better. We have the children that you, that we, wanted to have. But soon they won't need us any more. All the years you have been coming and going, I have been here. I have lifted them in and out of the car and the bath and their snowsuits and I have chopped food and fried it and wiped up all this mess, quite literally wetting a dish-cloth and running it over the dirty surfaces. But that's not needed any more.

She stops with the last cup in her hand, the dishwasher empty and ready to be filled up again. *That's not needed as much* sounds more level. It is important not to show rage, or anything that could be interpreted as rage; I do not feel rage, Anna thinks. It's not rage but sorrow, right?

Of course the children still need us, but soon they will have left home, in seven years or in a quarter of an hour, and all this time I have been here, in this room. It's empty now. Right? No. I can't say that, that's too emotional, too silly, and anyway, it isn't true, there's aeons to go. Maybe it's not emotional enough.

How about if I try this: all the time invested in ground support, it's free now. I have to think of myself. I have to be allowed to be myself? She lets the words fall silent in her mouth. She gets down a packet of ground almonds from the shelf and a knife that can cut courgette into strips.

The conversation does not happen, the days continue to have a content that is fixed in form. It can be pulled from the washing machine and hung on a line.

Anna takes photographs, or reminds Jens that something needs photographing. Later, she will be the one who owns the albums containing the explanations for all those mental images. The one who remembers dates and the anecdotes associated with each season.

Anna paints her cheeks but not her lips, and pulls her hair back from her forehead. Harry stands in the doorway, swaying back and forth on his heels, and watches her as she looks at herself in the mirror. She has been looking at herself almost all day, every mirror telling her something new.

In the morning she was in the department store, holding up a dress that had no discernible shape in front of her rather distinct shape. She held it up in front of the mirror. It looks comfortable, feels sleek, has an appealing colour, she thought.

She has begun to see women move through the city in wide coats. Anna thinks of the wide coats now. She wonders if the women wearing them have reached a consensus about what is attractive, with a different expectation about silhouette, or if they've lost their grip on all consensus: how else to explain this free formal language that doesn't show one's weight.

In the afternoon, in the hallway, when she took off her shoes, she thought, it is possible to not put on these shoes, or at least to choose a skirt that is less narrow. The thought was a game, just a game, like when the children play with the door, something you have to nag them to stop doing, an irritating habit, an openness without function. She got up again after pressing her thumb into the arch of her foot.

The scent of her foot was sour on her finger, she washed her hands. She pressed her thumb into her neck, she made some dough. Now it is evening, one more mirror, yet another angle, new colour in her cheeks. Harry's hair needs cutting. Anna raises her eyebrows at him in the mirror: Did you want something? He doesn't look happy. But children must learn they cannot always be the centre of attention.

She remembers when he was younger and he used to come and lie beside her at night. We can't be having this, she used to think, it's so hot. She has never been able to sleep with someone holding her. But every night he would ask if she wanted to lie on his arm. His arm that was so small and weak and still is.

Harry is eleven years old. He has become too independent to respond to gestures, he needs to be told in words, so she adds these words in a clear voice: Did you *want* something? She steps into her heels and suddenly he is even smaller. She puts a hand on his head as she leaves the room. Somewhere along the hallway he turns off, perhaps to his room, because when she reaches the upper landing and glances back he is no longer there.

She hears the babysitter and Hedda downstairs. Good lord, didn't she ring the doorbell? What kind of way to behave is that? Anna turns back and finds Harry sitting with his Lego on the floor of his room, the Lego he gets out when he's not allowed to play computer games, the computer games that are not a book, that are not a good way to pass the time, and the Lego that is not out in the fresh air either but is a compromise. She bends down and sees him light up; words start up towards her.

Everything almost goes black for a second and she hears far-off how he stammers out his description of the spaceship it will become. Super cool, he says, a phrase she dislikes. She must have bent down too quickly. She has to put her palms on the floor and then her knees, and in the end she is sitting beside him on the rug, quietly arranging the pieces he is not using. He talks and talks and she arranges and arranges. Soon she finds herself putting the pieces back in the box, then she is interrupting him and telling him it's time to tidy up, that he can't be spreading his junk all over the floor every five minutes and if she has to tell him one more time she'll be taking the damn Lego and throwing it out.

And he, like everyone else, has long since stopped believing that I'll ever do anything, Anna thinks, that I will ever be of any consequence, she thinks, and he keeps building and does not respond.

Right, that's it, Anna says. She gets up. I'm not telling you again. And she takes the box of Lego into the hallway and puts it on a high shelf in the wardrobe there and then she goes downstairs and tells the babysitter how great it is that she's there and sadly Harry's been a real pain so no more Lego for him tonight.

Harry comes down the stairs, quickly, and he says sorry and that he'll tidy up and that he promises. Anna cannot give in now, but then Jens comes along and he looks at her in a way that makes her feel like he can see some of those things that must not be allowed to show between them, and he puts his arm around Harry, she sees that too, and he says to Harry, I'm sure you can figure things out after Mamma and I have left.

And then he says, Harry, give Mamma a hug now and Harry does and Anna gets her coat and then they leave and on the drive she realizes she has not said goodbye to Hedda so she has to go back and Hedda is already sitting in front of the TV but Anna can't bring herself to say anything, so she just gives her a kiss and tells her to be good. She can hear Harry's voice upstairs, a high treble, happy, he is speaking even faster but it sounds like he's playing with someone, it sounds like he keeps pausing to listen to what someone else is saying.

Anna keeps trying different therapists, all men. She tells them her memories, or what has replaced the memories. She is often uncertain whether what she is telling them has happened or not. She might have dreamed it or made it up. Or maybe, she thinks, everything has happened and the alienation I feel is a way of getting some distance. She does not know for sure and since she can't tell her therapists she has a habit of lying about things, they are unable to help her.

Sometimes this dilemma makes Anna feel very, very ill. Sometimes she thinks the reverse: my ability to see through the myth that truth exists makes me clear-sighted. Everything is relative, Anna thinks then, feeling cynical, and therefore adult, and therefore intelligent.

Regardless of the degree of truth, it feels good to say it, to hear one's voice rising, falling, breaking, and think that this indicates something. It gives her life: to let her face reflect different kinds of movement and to be asked how what she says makes her feel. She sits on assorted grey armchairs on assorted semi-antique rugs and gazes through white curtains overlooking small courtyards. And as she sits there, the words come.

She hears herself talk and sees her reflection in the darkening glass of the window and thinks she looks deeply moved, that she must be their most interesting patient, that the therapist will surely think of her later and want to sleep with her to comfort her but that she is inaccessible in her sorrow.

That is why she talks about Mother with a calm distance, never stumbling over her words, and why she talks about Father with tenderness and gives them the whole diagnosis so they will understand she does not relate to what happened in a childish way.

She talks about Jens in a reasoning tone and about the children with quiet earnestness, she talks about them as the most valuable thing in her life, because that is how she wants to be remembered, as unimpeachable in her fundamental loyalty to the ones she has sacrificed everything for. She implies that when it comes to quarrels, it takes two to tango.

She talks for around forty minutes and afterwards she is always a little too hot and a little too red in the face. It feels like she has eaten, like it used to feel when she still ate, or as though she has drunk many cups of coffee. As though she were moved by her own words.

The memories she shares are always the same: they are, as she herself puts it on one occasion, like stones polished to a high shine. By that she presumably means that the retelling of these real or illusory memories involves a renunciation in which something that is actually quite tragic is transformed into a good story. An anecdote, a fun anecdote that denotes strength or a humorous one that denotes vulnerability.

*

Winter comes, they head for the heat. Anna has brought a book one ought to have read long ago. In the heat she cannot make sense of the words. She must look in the direction of the children, who are snorkelling under the surface, they must feel her eyes on them when they stick their heads up. She is forced to look in that direction; she thinks that's what being a mother is.

She thinks about the white fabric around the bed and she thinks, I ought to buy something like that to take home, and she thinks, I ought not to be so materialistic. She thinks about Jens reading on the sunlounger beside her. She thinks about how many calories there might be, or not be, in shellfish or in pineapple.

A credible existence is not just a matter of appearances. It is also a composite of all the small gestures, the choice of colours and the book on the bedside table. Being oneself is not something that comes naturally. Becoming oneself is a science; it requires consideration, decades of study. Anna folds down pages in magazines, she affixes images in colour order, she saves the names of ceramicists, she saves images of sturdy planters.

Once, long ago now, Jens never would have read on a beach, he never would have used the time in that way. He would have lain sleeping with his hand on the small of her back; other times were for reading. Anna used to wear sunglasses and he used to catch her eye anyway, as though it were worth catching, a real catch. All she was expected to do was to smile so imperceptibly that he slid the frames down and looked her deep in the eye. Anna thinks she should not be thinking about it, she should be living in the moment, she should let herself be rocked by the splashing of the waves, that's how it should feel now, she thinks. That kind of calm, she should say later, that's what makes it so luxurious, the calm there, the quietness. We're not really ones for luxury, she says later, but the calm is something I'm happy to pay for.

Anna cannot be boring, so it must be Jens who is boring. Anna cannot love a boring man, so she cannot love Jens. Anna cannot be married without love, so she must want a divorce. She looks at men on the metro, on the street, in magazines. She looks at all the ones who seem like they could take her to other kinds of dinners, dinners where she might say something fascinating about humanity; the kind of men who wear overcoats of a certain cut.

Then she dismisses them because of their height, their occupation, their income. She returns home and measures Jens's shoulders against hers. They make her look fragile. And it will be Christmas soon, you can't get divorced just before Christmas.

Anna cannot look her longing away; she turns away from herself. She worries about the state of the world, about the children's grades. She is not superficial, she knows what is important. She looks at friends whose children drowned, or who have developed a double chin, and she feels lucky. She's so brave, Anna says about someone else, and adds, After all, health is the most important thing.

Anna cannot afford to get a divorce: their living expenses are too high for her income alone. The reason she is not better paid must be because she has sacrificed herself for her family. To sacrifice oneself for one's family is to give the children stability.

Not leaving has value in itself. Anna is not the type to give up, to rush naively onwards. Anna has values, and because Anna has values, it is not her financial circumstances that stop her getting divorced. She buys lambswool sweaters to emphasize these values. She paints her nails with pale polish, she puts very small diamonds in her ears to show off her enduring ideals.

Summer again. Anna kneels and digs through the cool box. The children eat their slices of melon, and pink juice dribbles over their fingers. They might as well wash themselves off in the sea. Harry gets it into his head to shout, Blood! Blood! at the pink juice, behaviour he is at least three years too old for, and then they both run: up the sand to eat a piece of melon and then down into the waves screaming, Blood! Up again, and then the cry: Blood! The beach is almost empty, they are not disturbing anyone else. But they ought to be too old for this. Blood! Harry calls, and the gulls shriek at the same pitch.

Jens follows the children with his eyes, taking ever-longer pauses in his reading. Anna sees him looking not because he has to but because he wants to. She sees that he is not irritated by the fact they are acting younger than they are. She sees that Jens sees the sea, the sky, the sand and the children playing, and she sees that in seeing this, Jens forgets her.

*

Anna maintains a balance between being in control of the diary and not counting the days. Counting the days only leads to unhappiness. She does not count the number of times she has stuffed laundry into the dryer.

I am present, she thinks, and closes her eyes, stirring the bolognese. Her thoughts seldom get further than that, seldom beyond presence itself. She has been reading about presence like she used to read about attachment.

The goal with presence is not to feel frustration about nothing happening. Life could be different; one should accept this. Life should not cause one's palms to itch as it does now.

Another summer. The heat is oppressive, the melon is gone. Anna writes letters just beyond the edge of the towel. She writes *F* and she writes *X*, she writes big round *O*s, one after the other. She wakes, disoriented, half an hour later. No catastrophe has occurred, there is no lifeguard rushing out into the waves. Jens did not even notice she was asleep.

Anna thinks she would like to hit Jens and tests out the thought. When Jens has sex with her, she struggles not to bite him, struggles even more because he doesn't bite her. She has to clench her jaw as hard as she can to resist making her move while she has the chance, while she is in close proximity to forearms, to stop herself pushing her throat in between his teeth, under the palms of his hands. Anna turns onto her side, she knows her hipbone is clearly visible like that, that it casts a shadow and that it comes out well in photos.

*

Efforts are made, now there is time for effort, now the children take themselves to their activities. As instructed, Anna and Jens lick each other, and they sit opposite each other at a table and in armchairs opposite each other in a therapist's office.

In couples therapy they conduct constructive conversations intended to bring them closer to one another and they argue in the right way and they show each other respect, in the first person. They reach agreements and look at circles the therapist has drawn showing how communication works and they exhale into each other's ears.

The aim is: to find time for one another and to find time for themselves. The intention is to cherish what can be cherished. Anna thinks she owes Jens a little tenderness, if for no other reason than that he looks so tired now and the hair is falling out of his head.

Anna accompanies Jens to Oslo and they go to the opera together, an activity that does not come naturally to either of them. But however much effort she makes she cannot shed her skin, cannot turn herself into what is needed: something new to herself, or something forbidden to him. In the hotel room they try having Jens tell her to take her clothes off. She does not feel the words in her body. She is on autopilot doing as he tells her, lying on the bed as he tells her and closing her eyes.

He ties her up right away, without the merest flourish. Displeasure courses through her: for god's sake, she can hear his breathing. She can feel his knees against her sides as he ties the knots. He doesn't even tie them tight enough. She turns her head away, in spite of her closed eyes. She wishes vaguely she were somewhere else, or that it might start hurting soon. She tries to picture a large room lined in marble with people in masks, but the image will not stick, the present forces its way through, in. The fumbling.

She knows he is barely looking at her as she lies there, he has seen all this before, from this precise angle. A tear is already running down her cheek. It feels unreal that she should be crying, and yet it is a release, a confirmation. If she cries and he has tied her to a bed, that must mean they are really doing this now. That they are capable of seeing it through.

If only it were not so difficult from a practical point of view. The ropes are too thick and do not quite seem to want to bind to her wrists. Now one match after another is breaking in his hand as he tries to melt the wax. And from a purely practical perspective, how is he going to be able to reach around and spank her when he has tied her down on her back? Fucking hell. She sneaks a look and sees him standing with a spare rope in his hands and wants nothing but to go home. Or to a bar, where there will be a possibility of suggesting all this but in a version without scent or sound.

Anna discovers a new way of cooking aubergine – she roasts it for a long time in its skin, then she drizzles a little oil over it and serves it with parmesan. She reads in the paper that redoing your kitchen is a fool's game. Anna experiments with agreeing, then experiments with not agreeing. She tries to make the aubergine thing with pumpkin instead. It's delicious.

*

Summer comes around again. Anna lies on her stomach in the sand, facing the sea with her chin in her hand. She follows the children with her gaze, she is there with them every second, every second they are there; sometimes they go on adventures of their own, and she reads her book.

Jens has fallen asleep with his face on the pale pink pages of the finance section. Anna draws in the sand with a rough, dry piece of straw. She draws letters, rubs them out with her hand, draws them again.

She jerks out of sleep, don't lose focus now: the children are splashing in water up to their knees. *Closer to the beach!* she signals to them. You never know when a current could sweep through. When her head clears and reality creeps back in, she remembers they are not her children, she does not need to worry about them, they are someone else's children, small, wearing T-shirts against the sun, hair cut into fringes. Her children are the bigger ones, the ones who can swim or nod off with a book, who have cycled off to play tennis.

One Saturday in February Anna boils meat for borscht. Braising steak simmers slowly in salted water with white peppercorns and bay leaves. It needs to cool quickly, so she carries the heavy cast-iron pot out to the veranda. She places another heavy pan on top to protect it from animals. It will be there overnight.

On Sunday morning she wakes early, at half past four. Perhaps she heard something. Jens is flat on his back. Anna turns on her side and lays a hand on Jens's hands, clasped on his chest. He does not wake, but lays a thumb over her hand.

PART TWO

The force of sexual attraction is determined according to objective criteria, rated on numerical scales. But the ultimate proof of a woman's power to attract is that someone wishes to possess her.

A woman who is possessed by no one but herself eats an apple of air, nothing but pantomime.

Anna sits in the back seat of the taxi beside Jens, who is looking at his phone. She wonders now, as she sometimes does, whether he has a mistress, but she does not think so. There is nothing to indicate that he is tense or full of anticipation or particularly happy or unhappy. He rarely stands there smiling at nothing in particular. There is no furtiveness. There is not even furtiveness.

They pull up outside the correct house, the taxi stops, Anna hunches her shoulders inside her coat while Jens pays and then looks at his phone again to check the door code. The wind is blowing off Lake Mälaren. Anna can see it in the aura around the street lamps. It reminds her of a painting she can't quite remember, by someone whose name she can't recall.

It annoys her that she cannot remember, otherwise she might have said *This evening's a real ___ evening*. A real Eugen evening? A real Hopper evening? A real Rothko evening? She tries, but nothing fits. Perhaps, she thinks, I should mention instead that I've started forgetting names? And that I tried on some glasses this week? I never remember how many scoops of coffee I've put in the machine, that's a real handicap. She pictures the scene, sees the other guests' warm smiles in response to her unassuming self-effacement.

Anecdotes told over dining tables that have been extended to fit more place settings are the space in which to show oneself off. Certain flourishes of the hand are also permitted, as well as certain unexpected colour combinations and cuts, asymmetric necklines. Anna must fill these moments with as much content as possible. As much of her interior as possible must be packaged in these outward symbols so she appears to be a live individual, a woman with a lively face, someone who experiences life keenly.

Exaggeration is always required, an anecdote without exaggeration is held up by… what? Reality? The exaggerations must be obvious, so they do not make her look like she takes herself seriously.

Anna can talk about Barthes using the correct pronunciation, or avoid talking about Barthes entirely so as to be a little less predictable. She can fling uncorroborated provocations into the conversation to watch them crackle into life: that she prefers not to read female authors, that she prefers Catholicism, that she prefers to take taxis, that she has always preferred a man who can't find his way around the children's sock drawers. That she would prefer a cocktail. That stockings and suspenders are as comfortable as tights. That she's not hungry, or the reverse, that she is hungry.

All this assumes that the men in the room are in the mood to laugh. If they are in a different mood, Anna keeps her mouth shut, expectant. The anecdotes remain there, ready to be spoken when needed.

The taxi drives off. They are left on the street with no conflict lines drawn. And yet it is so clear it does not need to be stated: Jens knows Anna thinks it is taking him a long time to find the door code and that the wind is blowing off Lake Mälaren. Anna knows that her shoulders, hunched to her ears, are saying *I'm so damn tired of this and it's only a matter of time, you know*. She says it again by calmly opening the door to the building and walking, poised, up the stairs instead of crowding into the tiny lift. Jens's steps behind her say that this will pass, this mood, which makes her neck flush, like a child who's been told off.

They ring the doorbell when they get to the right floor and wait for someone to open up. When Anna hears steps from within, she nestles against Jens's shoulder. As it should, automatically, his hand finds the small of her back. He is reliable in company. She curves her back a little, pushing so imperceptibly against his palm that only he can feel the clench of her muscles: nothing is visible to an outside observer. A movement that is an echo of all the times she has arched her lower back and pressed herself against him in bed; it's in her bones, the idea that this curve is sexual, and what is sexual is intimate, and intimacy is we won't argue tonight, intimacy is the phone can wait until we're back in the taxi and no one is looking and I can stare bitterly out of the window over Traneberg Bridge. That curve holds all this.

The first time Anna sees Ivan in real life, he is standing with his back half towards her in that hallway. And the first time Ivan sees her, she has Jens's chin with its carefully considered stubble against her throat: a token of playfulness between them, as though she were the kind of woman who is soft and warm after more than twenty years together, the sort of permissive woman who doesn't argue when you are out for dinner and have forgotten the door code but smiles indulgently and strokes your cheek regardless. Ivan is fresh from a divorce. He wishes someone had been as warm with him as Anna seems to be with her husband; he thinks he would have been a better person then.

Anna scans her memory. Has she seen his face before, have they exchanged greetings somewhere? All these people passing by; she often claims to have a poor memory for faces, she often jokes that she has such a terrible eye for detail, as though life were full of new people to mix up.

When they introduce themselves and go from standing angled away from each other to standing face to face it strikes her that she recognizes him from photos in his books and in interviews. Ivan is established. Established somewhere in the borderlands of prose and poetry, between philosophy and its political implications.

She knows she has claimed to have read those of his books educated people are meant to have read, and to some extent it is true, she did once read something. She knows she sat in a park one afternoon and a man came up to her and asked what she was reading. She knows how the light filtered through the branches near the observatory and she knows she was able to hold up the cover dismissively and sink back into the words, her chest thrust forward in the event he should glance back over his shoulder. The image is absolute, like the memory of a scent. She believes the scent is Ivan's.

Ivan represents all the men who have seen her with a book, as well as the multifaceted men he has sketched, their grave sins and the grand thoughts they have had. He is all the men on the street and the metro who have looked thoughtful, all the ones who have held on with large hands as the carriage sways. All this idealized masculinity obscures the possibility of another kind of analysis, one rooted in him as a real individual, one that could never be overlooked in anyone else: the shirt sleeve that is a little too wide around his narrow elbow, the collar badly ironed just there. Those strands of hair at his neck, that suggestion of an overbite that might conceal a wad of snus.

It must be a sign, recognizing someone immediately, Anna thinks, not caring that she didn't recognize him immediately. If she thinks about the cut of his shirt at all, it is to think: it wouldn't be like that any more, not with me.

When he says his name she recognizes his voice too. From readings on the radio as she stood at the sink in the summerhouse and cut strawberries into the children's yogurt and heard that voice, the note of reflection, the sound that is public property in some sense and yet, because it speaks so slowly, intimate.

She feels her throat flush from her breastbone to her chin and even across her shoulders, though differently to how it did in the stairwell. Anna and Jens go on circulating, as one does, but her throat stays flushed. For the rest of the evening she is conscious of a tension in every part of her that is in his line of sight: a clenching behind her ears, the cramping of a little, unknown muscle below her left shoulder blade.

Further off, in different circumstances, she will note how bony his chest is, the belly beneath it soft, a growth. That his shoulders slope, that his nails have vertical furrows and have hardened and yellowed at the corners. That his teeth are darker further up by the gum and are worn in certain places. That his lips have dried into depressions where he has dug his teeth in and that in the creases of his face forgotten stubble glitters silver and red.

Later she will be close, so close she will be able to count the pores on the wings of his nose, to stroke his temples until the longer hairs lie flat. His ears contain dark yellow wax: if he were her child and her child were small she would scoop it out with her little fingernail. He has smooth dark hairs on his shoulders and in the hollow of his chest. Not many, but they are there.

She will pretend not to see the grey fluff that has accumulated in his navel. She will follow the trail down towards his boxers: the elastic at the waist will be frayed and greyish, the legs shapeless. The fabric will be damp from the warmth of his groin, the scent of detergent will seem stronger. She will rub her cheek against the worn cloth and she will think of all the times his wife must have washed these boxers, and then she will shut out all thought of washing machines: she must be swept up in the moment.

Further down, the top of his socks will have cut into his calves even though they are skinny; the marks will be red against his white skin. Beneath his socks, the feet with their dry, cracked heels and the white traces of fungus on the nails. He will almost lose his balance when he makes to lie over her: a sign of ageing, or perhaps because of the wine, or simple bad luck.

None of this will have the chance to occupy space inside her. She cannot detect the soft parts of Ivan, she does not allow soft parts in an object.

Attraction is a dramaturgically flawless construction, from hunger to habituated swallowing. Like all constructions, it has its own internal logic: for attraction to exist, there must be two separate entities, as well as a surface for them to travel over. There should be scope for a certain degree of dizziness, there should be the possibility of a damaging fall.*

For this reason, love is time-limited, measurable in seasons rather than lifetimes.

---

* *A marriage cannot offer this kind of emotional charge. For the married woman, infidelity is the most effective way of performing the function of desirability.*

When Anna was younger and used to fake orgasms, she would always make a noise. But she has set aside that extravagance. Now she effects instead a little pause in her breathing, then relaxes her muscles completely.

In this manner she can save the big gestures, such as tears or clutching the sheets, for sex she has after an argument or on holiday.

Anna becomes a mistress for reasons of efficiency, just as efficiency requires her to run on a treadmill, with her eyes forward. Towards the end her lungs burn.

At the table she is seated opposite Ivan. There are enough people there for several conversations to take place concurrently, but it is still him everybody is listening to. Later, Anna will wish she had understood the implications of this. That he was in a room where he was the most important person. That there were other, more important, more relevant people in another room, but he was in this one.

She does not notice this now, however; she is busy trying to find the phrase that will make him remember her as the most natural person in the room.

The woman to his right says she likes his books; she has openly assumed the role of admirer. The woman to the left says something a little daring, a little provocative. So she is to be the sceptic. It falls to Anna to be the cool one, the one you want to get to say something, the one from whom a smile must be drawn out.

It's no great challenge to be that woman, all she has to do is say nothing until her silence is established as something you want her to break, and to keep her eyelids lowered just enough. She takes off her bracelets and puts them on the tablecloth as though she had been longing to liberate herself, or as though she wished for some other symbols, some other man's symbols, around her wrists.

Now the wine is red. Anna moves the knife and fork with her hands. Ivan's voice continues, a kind of aural backdrop. She hears he is approaching what he has envisaged as the pivotal moment in his story. He does not use humour – he is not known for it – but a kind of drastic distancing that puts the listener in a hopeless situation. You can either agree with him about some untenable thing, in which case he will turn the argument against you, or you can object to his conclusion, in which case he will cling to it with a philosopher's stubbornness. The woman on the right falls into the first trap, the one on the left, the second.

Anna continues to say nothing, she knows how this conversation is constructed. The only way to win is to tuck her hair behind her ear and look away, as though everything were predictable, or as though she were thinking about something else.

*

Their eyes meet a number of times during the dinner. It would be stranger, more remarkable, if they had not. Looking away or not looking up would say something there is not yet any reason to say. So: their eyes meet again. Anna feels it in the pit of her stomach.

Anna notes that Ivan's eyes have a shape and a colour and the thought of the sea flashes through her mind. She is uplifted by this, by finally being able to compare someone else with the sea rather than always being the sea herself. She tries out the thought there at the table, thinks of the unrequited passion and how it would feel to worship, now she has finally met someone who might perhaps fit the role of god.

Ivan is holding forth on humanity. It is a long parenthesis in his ongoing narrative that is not particularly relevant, it comes close to destroying the story entirely. Anna knows she will need to say something soon, not yet but soon. But no, she thinks, I can raise my eyebrows a little more, raise them until he is talking to me directly, so he states his conclusion to me alone. Anna allows her eyebrows to lower in reward.

How does one move on from this? It is not difficult. Anna has a certain habit, Ivan apparently has a certain habit too. After all, they are adults. The steps are easy to follow. Lowering your voice half an octave when you at last begin to talk, speaking so quietly he leans forward. Saying nothing more after that. Remembering to look away. Excusing yourself after a while with *I feel like such a teenager tonight I want to smoke a cigarette*, and stepping out onto the cool balcony. Casting a look over your shoulder. Withdrawing in time to leave something to wonder over.

Lust transforms time by breaking it up. The lover can no longer be in the moment, she must always be in the moments she can imagine. At some point, earlier every day, a longing, manifested as restlessness, must force its way in.

The longing must fill time with something unattainable, the opposite to laundry. It must make one's hands tremble and fix the mind on something external during chores, so the woman avoids having to feel them being done by her hands, yet again.

On Tuesday Anna and Ivan exchange a few messages regarding a book they both enjoyed. They discover that one of them has not read absolutely all the books by that author and that the other must therefore lend a particular, unread book on a future occasion.

They agree to discuss the already-read book and other matters on Wednesday over coffee, which they drink while Anna's gaze falters and Ivan's self-confidence grows.

As they leave the cafe, which, Anna thinks, will soon be a cafe they visit regularly, their knees are trembling from caffeine and lust. Anna assumes their interaction must be something very special, that they've experienced something she regards as spiritual contact, since they've been talking for several hours. With each other, about things, with their clothes on, out of the house.

Later that evening, alone, she relives the nuances of the conversation. The ambiguous parts about chess and the rather obvious ones about how my husband doesn't quite understand the extent of my spiritual life, that towards the end my wife didn't understand, that everything felt empty.

She remembers how they looked at each other and especially how she looked away, she wonders at what angle he had seen her jaw and she is fascinated that the conversation never strayed beyond the bounds of propriety – exciting in itself.

They decide to go for a walk on Thursday. It is a way to exchange yet another book and is safe, because it's hard to have sex on a walk. Which may be true in theory, but nonetheless you can, you should – you must, anything else would be unreasonable! – sometimes pause, even on a walk, despite the cold, to consider that you feel different kinds of things and because you still have not touched each other, which is worth noting while standing still.

They look at the yellow post-war tower blocks on the other side of the water and giggle at how that must be Mälarhöjden or maybe Skärholmen and at the fact they do not know, that they are so wrapped up in themselves they do not really know where Skärholmen is.

Onwards, as a matter of course. Instead of these thoughts about Skärholmen or maybe Mälarhöjden leading to the appropriate conversation about social inequalities, it leads to yet another pause a few metres on.

Slowly but surely, the pauses exceed the steps and they find themselves standing beneath a pine tree looking at a fairly insignificant stretch of water as his thumb touches the indent behind her ear. Anna's legs shudder, they do not give way: she draws up her kneecaps; he has a crack in his lower lip. She leans towards the gap between his shirt buttons and takes a tentative sniff.

With the heightened awareness that comes from having

made out against a pine tree (adults, Anna laughs; you're so young, sighs Ivan), one returns home and the other goes out to meet a friend.

The barriers to them having sex, the sub-zero temperatures and the dog owners and the pine needles and the fact one is not quite so young as one once was, and all the coffee from their previous encounter, all these things converge in Anna's mind into an assumption that they did not have sex because they are too important, because this is something else. They have feelings that go deeper.

In short, Anna is convinced that this as-yet-unstated relationship is more than just a screw, that it must be because it involves him and he is who he is and she intends to be what he wants her to be.

If they'd had sex, everything would have been as it always is. There is a finite number of body parts and their use leads to a limited number of possible reactions. Sex is not that exciting once it actually happens.

If it, sex, had happened right away, everything would surely have been over and done relatively quickly, with the customary degree of rationality. During a long marriage no one can expect you to never, and so on.

But now, as a result of this and that, it takes several weeks before they manage to do the deed. In anticipation they do all the things that accompany it. Smoking more consistently again and listening to certain songs until one no longer hears them, waiting at a crossing and driving out along a road through the woods and parking in the shadows, following the curves beneath one another's cheekbones, laughing at (presumably) the same things, saying *I would like us to sleep together one night*, saying *I feel at home in your arms*, and other things Anna wonders if she has read or heard before in her own life.

The woman's relation to men, as a collective, is cyclical and repeatable ad infinitum, ad nauseam.

Penetration and the associated markers of belonging are, by their very nature, repetitions of prior experiences. Some prefer to conduct them repeatedly with the same type of individual. Others prefer to move in a new direction, between age categories or occupations, or in exceptional cases between social classes.

These differences can be explained by disposition, by daddy issues, by what the woman seeks to process on an individual level.

Convincing oneself that what one is doing again is something one has not done before is a balancing act that requires a high degree of self-censorship and self-suggestion. This may explain why women, who are so well trained in these particular forms of egoism, are often said to be better at interpersonal communication.

The opening weeks of the relationship are a strain. Anna cancels meetings and keeps herself awake at night to think of Ivan. She adjusts her hair and make-up depending on how much he wants to pull it and how much his stubble scratches her cheeks. She asks about his childhood and the films he has seen and about guitar picks, and she swaps to a different brand of the cigarettes that have now become an explicit habit rather than a rare occurrence.

Time not spent on the above is spent with Jens. She feels a need to calm him, which finds expression alternately in rage and in a tenderness that, if he were not so oblivious, she thinks, ought to make him suspicious.

The husband, the lover and the mistress presuppose each other. Anna needs Jens so she can be Ivan's mistress, just as she needed her children so she could be a mother. For Ivan to provide gratification, Jens must a) exist and b) be kept in the dark. It is this tension that leads to pain, it is pain that defines the pleasure; the reason being that an urge acted upon in the light of day loses its meaning.

The existence of Jens, the lies and dissimulation, add a frisson that, like horse-riding or other, similar sports, is at once exhausting and, through the exhaustion, liberating.

In time everything becomes routine, a routine that simplifies life. Anna finds breathing space outside of the bedroom and the respective intercourse/dinner locations. She reads the paper, she goes to the toilet. She undertakes everyday tasks with Jens without being interrupted by the phone, she sleeps with Ivan without forgetting her earrings.

They achieve – the three of them – an unspoken compromise between reality and ideal. Anna's need to pay for certain things, her portion of the mortgage instalments, for instance, is never discussed. Nor that she needs to brush her teeth. Ivan is not unreasonable, he does not require so much attention that she cannot comply with these obligations. Jens is with his boat, on a trip, at the office, tending the compost.

Anna tends to say that the advantage of creative work is that you don't exactly have to clock in. *It is a freedom I appreciate*, she tends to say then.

She uses her freedom to meet Ivan at times that suit him and to go into shops during lunch, ideally one of the food halls.

Today it is Wednesday and she has just left the cheese counter, where she chose a cheese that resembles Appenzeller but comes from another, less obvious place. Actually, it's even nuttier, the salesperson says. Anna proceeds to the meat counter, where she buys two beautifully aged steaks, not too large – that can be disgusting. She swings by the counter that sells fine chocolates.

She talks to the staff about quality and aroma and flavour. They recognize each other, and can indulge in a joke. The staff know Anna's husband is a real foodie. She does not need to tell them about the dinner she and her husband are going to eat; she is here so often everyone knows this is typical for her, that this Wednesday is not special. That they are simply the kind of couple who like to do these things for each other. Don't all couples do the same?

Anna takes the escalator up and steps out onto the square. Jens is in Oslo tonight. On her way to the office she drops the food into a rubbish bin.

On Tuesdays, when Ivan is in town to meet his publisher or go to a bar with a friend, to visit a bookshop or go to the cinema, they find time to meet. The encounters themselves follow a clear pattern too, pressed for time. It's the lack of time that makes the whole thing feel a little truncated, Anna thinks. It is absolutely not the case that the routine is making the intensity ebb away. Heavens, what kind of person would that make me? Anna wonders. Someone who never feels anything?

They drink coffee at the usual place. Today there is no time to drive anywhere because Ivan has surströmming night at Olof's and has to go and buy the drinks.

They talk about Ivan's work. He's worried about the times they are living in, that they are capitalist. Anna nods. His face is recognizable! she thinks.

He says he doesn't get the media's hard tone these days, and she thinks that their hands are almost touching across the tablecloth but not quite. He says he wishes there could be more consideration, more stillness, and she thinks the other customers are probably wondering who she is and why they are talking in such low voices.

This thought is so charged that the scene almost becomes black and white. She feels the silence sharpening her profile. She feels the silk of her skirt against her thighs and feels that it is silk – what else? – and that the image is iconic.

The language Ivan uses has not changed for many years, but his words have taken on new meanings, become loaded in ways he is not aware of. When he participates in public discourse it leads to misunderstandings, skirmishes where he has not realized a boundary has been erected. The new modes of debate, their rules, have been drawn up in rooms he does not enter, rooms that require another knowledge of technology than that which he possesses.

Ivan still hears his voice the way it used to sound, not through the ears of the listener. He is surprised, therefore, that others find it off-key. His surprise passes daily into frustration, the frustration sharpening his metaphors until they become pure provocation. He is deeply entrenched in a conflict with his times.

Anna is a white space on the map, a place to rest, a place where he still holds the map in his hands, allowing him to call her body a landscape without her taking offence.

Anna is young enough to trust him and too old to question everything. He can explain politics so she understands it in a new way, he explains it on an ideological level, giving an overview, a history of the ideas.

He can explain which thoughts are significant and which are pretentious nonsense, and he explains the present time, how it underestimates some people and overestimates others. He explains what is a valid argument and what is illogical. He explains what is worth reading and what is not worth reading, what is likely to have staying power and what is best understood as commercial trash.

She starts to carry different books than she used to and stops reading the reviews in the paper, since they understand nothing anyway. Ivan says he has no TV, and she says that sounds like a relief.

Ivan explains what one might laugh at a little, and he explains how it makes him feel, how it wounds him, when she laughs in the wrong place. He explains how the light and the climate affect him and he explains the need to have a woman, what a woman means to a man, what a woman means when he is expressing himself. Then he explains that the times they are living in do not understand these things, that society has become crass and hard and unable to see, in the right way, the value in things and so on, and that this is what he is writing his next book about.

And she is the woman, the woman who was, the woman she has shown him can still exist, even today.

The alternative to the cafe is to meet in the car and drink coffee from paper cups before having sex in more or less uncomfortable positions. For Anna this adds yet another dimension to their relationship: it is not comfortable, it is not about intercourse being practical.

They never mention hotel rooms. For Anna it is a question of aesthetics: she can't screw at the Scandic, that's a line she won't cross.

There is going home, and there is going home. On days when it feels like the latter, Anna takes the metro, actively closing her eyes and wondering who sees her close them. She goes to the supermarket and buys what is needed and hopes that other people notice how little is needed, that she is ascetic, not someone who buys crisps.

She walks along streets lined with leafless trees, through piles of leaves, towards home. The tarmac is cracked and full of holes. Jens is always getting himself worked up about this and about how close to one another the cars park on the street. He has talked to the neighbours about paying out of their own pockets to have the street resurfaced, but the discussion ran out of steam, as though it was hard to decide where they would stop, how far they should go with the tarmac.

The gate squeaks. The house is quiet. The cleaner comes on Fridays, every Friday, but she has already left: it's almost six. Anna puts the post in its usual place. She puts the shopping bag on the counter and lays the flowers next to it.

First she will unpack the shopping. Then she will unload the dishwasher. She thinks it a little odd, and always says as much to Jens, that the cleaner does not do it, given what they pay her. They often talk about whether or not Anna should contact the cleaning firm about this but have not yet settled on a plan of action.

Anna is going to trim the flowers. Then she will put them in the vase she always uses and place it on the table in the living room. Even without the cleaner the table would be totally clean. The children are grown.

Her relationship with Ivan, their physical infidelity, is subject to logistical concerns. They cannot be allowed the lulls that characterize marriage. Because it takes place on well-defined occasions, Anna can afford to be extreme. She can let go, safe in the knowledge that her abandon will not need to be maintained. The end of the encounter sets a limit; Ivan's prior arrangements, the supermarket's opening hours.

This is how the terms of her life differ, now she defines herself as Ivan's lover, from the time when she was primarily a mother. Motherhood continued inescapably, around the clock, year in, year out. It had to consist unrelentingly of happiness and of smiling with her voice at Harry, who didn't want to eat his potatoes. Now Anna has to swallow semen with the same eager look, the same smiling tone. But since she knows she will soon be able to close her eyes in solitude and allow her facial muscles to relax, she is able to be more convincing than she ever was in motherhood.

Anna moves through the room and finds the light that most flatters her, she practises in anticipation of him seeing her and turning what he sees into art.

She carries a notebook with her and experiments with drawing in it, then realizes this is ridiculous and tries to write in it instead, but there is an accidental rhyme on the second line and that doesn't look good.

She puts down the notebook, picks up Auden's collected poems and moves the bookmark around in it. She cleans her nails with the bookmark. She nods off in the chair.

In the evenings Anna pretends to herself that it is the weariness of the day and not some other weariness she feels in her joints, head and throat. Then she thinks that perhaps it's cancer, or that the children have cancer, or, even better, Jens.

Jens has fried a small cut of meat. The frying pan is tipped casually into the sink. He is eating the meat in front of the TV with his laptop beside him on the coffee table. There is a bottle of red wine and a Japanese bowl containing flakes of salt too. Jens has a spreadsheet open. The news is on TV.

There are noises coming from somewhere in the house. He probably doesn't really think about them, she thinks, those ordinary little sounds of me tidying up the remains of the day. How I wash the cast-iron frying pan, put the dirty clothes into the basket, pinch dead leaves from the pelargonium. No sudden movements, nothing that draws attention to itself. But he doesn't hear me doing this either, Anna thinks with every sound she makes.

*

When Jens and Anna met, she knew he didn't see her beauty, not as she had intended for it to be seen. He saw certain obvious attributes, but even then he had no eye for detail. He is colour-blind, and that means she has to paint with excessively bold shades to get through to him. She knows he likes things that are incompatible with her variant of beauty: for daytime a sportiness that does not suit her; after dark a banality that catches in her throat.

Anna knows that the role of mistress requires her to stay up to date with developments in pornography and to demonstrate enough knowledge of the poses and gestures of classical art to paraphrase them. She must vary her expressions of devotion and aggression, her lipstick, within the bounds of what Ivan finds desirable and/or forbidden.

Being Ivan's mistress gives her an opportunity to change her clothes, her hairstyle too. His vocation calls for a more muted colour palette, for the lack of body that requires one to be thinking always of one's body, to make it smaller, more refined. Her manifestation of Ivan's renowned intellectual stature is to be so little body that her body is the first thing one notices.

Nothing in my appearance is simplistic, she thinks these days when she sees herself in the mirror or mirrored surfaces. She looks natural, and it is this consciousness that she implies and contradicts with a wave of her hand. It fits with his ideas: his ideas are an appropriate accessory in her hand, a different kind of ring.

Ultimately, Anna looks as though she is thinking of something else but thinking about it as if she is in a painting by a very early modernist: late Schjerfbeck, for instance.

She has put away her dainty earrings and bought cardigans with more drape and less structure.

Yet another Friday. Anna opens the dishwasher. First do the boring things, the dishes, then the fun things, the flowers. It's not full but I'm in the habit of putting it on in the morning after breakfast, she imagines herself saying, as if to an audience. She imagines the audience being fascinated by her wrists, how thin they are and yet how competent. It's not nice to come home to a kitchen that smells of stale washing-up, she says. It's the least you can do, to make sure the breakfast has been tidied away, that the beds are made, she imagines herself saying with a smile.

The dishwasher is empty. The shopping put away. Anna trims the tulips, fifty of the same colour, otherwise there's simply no point. At first she holds them in her arms, then she arranges them in the vase. She sets the vase on the table.

The flowers are not really white, not pure white, they have a greenish tone in the centre. Anna thinks it is important to buy yourself flowers. And the tulip season is so short. And they are so beautiful when they start to nod, almost like works of art, Anna thinks, though she would never say that, it has been said so many times before.

Anna leaves the kitchen and goes into the living room. She feels the earth in the plant pots. She rearranges the sofa cushions – there are some things the cleaner just does not understand: they should be the other way, so as not to look arranged.

Anna does not look at the wall where the TV is. She loathes the TV, has begun to loathe it actively instead of simply not understanding why it needs to be so large. The one upstairs should be enough, but Jens wants two. And why does it have to be so ugly. Why does life have to be so ugly. Anna swallows and looks at the art on the other wall. It is real art. That is to say that it is not too figurative and it is painted with oils on canvas. They are collectors, she and Jens.

Anna has chosen the books on the shelves for the names of the authors and chosen the chair for its designer; the elongated arc of the lamp is easily recognized, as is the surface of the table. They are collectors: Anna has a passion and Jens thinks it looks nice. The silver candelabras are a counterpoint. They are not new: the silver is an heirloom. Anna knows a thing or two about antiques; Jens likes to light candles when they have guests.

Just before their guests arrive fifteen minutes later than the agreed time, Jens goes around lighting the candles while Anna finishes up in the kitchen so she can be surprised at the stove with a glow in her cheeks.

Jens does not act nervously when Anna enters the room, does not angle his screen away. He has no code on his phone and he leaves his laptop open. There is no evidence he has met someone. Every time he travels to Oslo he calls home.

If there were furtiveness there might be something to rage against, Anna thinks, looking at her face in the mirror, in the circle she clears in the steam. As it is now, I have nothing to complain about, no reason to be angry.

So she is not angry. She brushes her hair. She switches to a new toothbrush. She wipes the tap clean. Jens lets life go on in the background. He busies himself by going in and out of doors, shooting animals and portioning out their flesh, by following the news and letting down the sails and otherwise behaving in a way that provides a suitable backdrop.

His function is to keep on doing that, to keep being there in his predictability in the evenings when Anna is exhausted from the tensions of the day. At these times she feels grateful for his willingness to be boring, his responsible attention to routines she can break with.

The lover must be irrational. She must be femininity elevated to its conventional caricature. She should be obvious in her choice of undergarments and irresponsible in her choice of moments to call.

The lover must be sentimental. She must use verbs that connote tenderness and vulnerability, she must use adjectives like profuse and tired, to illustrate the most everyday occurrences. She should, for example, talk of a pain in her 'heart'. Yes, it is true, the lover really uses that word.

The lover must be extreme in her choice of terminology. Loving allows her to simultaneously use aphorisms and the most obvious terms for genitalia. The beloved breaks down her sense of grammar and her knowledge of aesthetic frameworks.

The lover must be naive. She must leave realism behind her, expended, so she can devote herself to an uninhibited romantic delusion. She must, for example, believe that constructions such as for all time, for ever *and* until I die *are chronological concepts.*

In fact, passion – the disproportionate interest in the

other that has the power to blind one to the wind blowing the grit up off the street – only exists as long as it is coming to an end.

Anna is preoccupied, preoccupied by her body and her emotions. In front of the mirror she tries to see what Ivan sees. It is for his sake that she twists and turns at different angles, in search of bruises or scratches or other physical marks. Because he finds new words for her hair colour and eye colour she has an excuse to consider them the way she did as a teenager, when she first discovered them.

Ivan gives her an excuse not to notice how Jens turns away, and at the same time an excuse to touch herself and to name herself, to use words such as *lotion*, to let her gaze rest there, on her body, not allowing it to drift towards concepts more complex than skin.

Anna often imagines the next conversation she and Ivan will have, rather vaguely perhaps: she has no specific ideas about the subject matter. But it will mean something, right? It will be something else?

At the office she sits at her desk, working and looking at the light over Lake Mälaren, thinking, I am now the kind of person who watches the light over Lake Mälaren; he has done that. Maybe I could put that light into words and say those words to him.

The words cannot be written on a computer, Anna thinks, a computer is not poetic, it's not a romantic thing. But when she takes out paper and pen she gets no further than writing *The Light over Lake Mälaren*, in cursive, then the thought muddies and her hand starts to draw petals, rounded in the centre and pointed at the tip, like tulips. She fills in the petals, drinks her coffee, then writes about a spa treatment and uses the words *treat yourself*, and then she starts a piece on greenhouses and uses the words *invest in a longer season* in the opening paragraph, and then it is time to go home.

After Ivan and Anna's lovemaking, which is important and deep in spite of its often comic aspects (the gearstick! the jogger in the woods! the sudden barking of a dog! a stain on the seat!), they talk, in accordance with her image of how love is.

Or it is mostly Anna who talks; Ivan is relatively quiet, surprisingly quiet in comparison to his public persona. But he does not contradict her when she says, for example, that next summer they could travel somewhere together, or when she says *I am yours*, or when she says *it would be impossible to go home if I couldn't look forward to us being together again.*

She pretends not to remember the anecdote he once related. Tell me what you think of Greece, she says.

The actual form their relationship takes is the price paid for the dream of it, for longing. Anna is in a constant state of disappointment over Ivan's shortcomings: mild or savage disappointment. To hide this from herself she says that she loves him, though she is not sure and, at moments, she is decidedly unsure. The fact of their not being able to see each other often, especially when this is a result of his commitments, makes Anna all the more sure she loves him. Otherwise she would not think so much about the fact that he cannot see her.

It does not matter to her that Ivan does not want to hear that she loves him, or at least not right now. I love you, Anna says, you are the one I've been waiting for all my life, she says. She does not care that he was not ready for that word. Was this supposed to be love? Ivan says to himself drowsily. Then he says, I guess that's what it's become.

To meet Anna's needs Ivan tries to say other things, things other than *I love you*. Things that would be more interesting: the words *I love you* are so tired. So instead of saying *I love you* he starts expounding on the subject of causality, losing Anna at some point; they both interpret this as being due to his intelligence, not because his reasoning is woolly.

He says *you interest me* and *you are unforgettable* and other things that are dangerous because they make her feel it's not just her breasts that matter. He sees my soul, she thinks.

I should let you go but I can't help myself, he says, and something about utilitarianism and something about Pound and something about Schrödinger, all of which she interprets as him saying it is what is inside her that he cannot resist, even if it often results in him touching her genitals through her clothing.

A touch through clothing is much more real than one without clothes. Anna interprets it as closeness. And yet she cannot stop herself wanting him to say those three ordinary words, the ones she supposes go along with spiritual contact and that kind of touching.

Her demands are formulated as questions and lead to overwhelming arguments – basically inconsequential and therefore fiery – with sophistries such as *What am I to you?* or *How often do I have to tell you that...*

The fights must be kept from Jens. So must the great intoxication she feels when the time comes for her to restore Ivan to favour. Jens's existence forces her to whisper, to whisper into the phone that is clamped to her ear under the apple tree, both during the argument and during the reconciliation, when the lens is focused on the most charged body parts, when their voices circle around biological terms made symbolic by the context. It gives the words more emphasis than those exchanged in previous arguments, in her legitimate relationship.

Ivan says that he loves Anna, her emotion tells him he must, the tremble in her voice, the rasp of her words.

Instead of registering his current reality, he remembers all the times he has persuaded himself that he is someone who could understand her, that she is someone who could understand him. That there is something to understand between people. That there is something that is not silence and is not *not* silence but a place poised in between. A place where he can be seen as relevant, with a depth that is otherwise obscured by trivialities. His about-turn here is human, trying to love what we have been given: something that loves us and demands a response.

*

Anna spends the days when she and Ivan do not meet – that is, every day except Tuesday – reading all his books again and writing long letters about her feelings.

She writes that the thought of him arouses her. At times she rehearses, with a vague hand, the actions she tells him she has carried out. But to reach true arousal she has to imagine a large room with marble benches, through which she is led on a leash by a man with no face. He leads her over to a group of people who slap her gently on the cheeks and backside. This she does not write.

She writes other things, to get a reaction, a contradiction or reassurance. She writes about her anxiety. She writes *It's my birthday on Monday. How long will I be what you want?* She writes *I can feel myself ageing, my body.* She writes things that can be interpreted as criticisms.

These letters elicit no reply, or even shorter replies than usual. She returns to the main focus: the description of her body and how it might react to him if he were there, instead of writing about her soul and how it reacts to the reality of him.

There are moments of solitude in crowds, when she can consider the fact that she is a mistress and what this does to her. One Saturday she goes from shop to shop, buying things, things mistresses ought to have. She thinks of the sales assistants speculating, assuming.

She sits amid the lunch smells and drinks a cup of black coffee and thinks of all the people inside the bistro, the fact that they are naked under their clothes. She leaves her coffee cup and steps out into the watery sunshine and goes to buy garments in cashmere.

The food still needs preparing, even though it's just the two of them. Anna wears out another pair of running shoes. Jens has a lot on at work as usual, she thinks with resolve. This itself is reassuring. Jens is a plumb line in Anna's life, a measure of the depth rather than the length of time. He can be followed down through time towards a sediment of shared memories and possessions. Through his past inevitability, he also anchors the future in this shared bedrock.

Now the children have reached their full heights and can no longer be measured, his function lies in always having existed. Ergo, Anna assumes, he will always continue to exist.

Between the beginning of a love affair and its end, moments that hold plenty of potential for dramatic statements, one finds a period of flat progression that is tiresome to live through as well as to describe.

The parties can conceal the boredom from one another by beginning to speak of scruples (religious, moral) or issues of trust (how do I know that you) or music (I always think of you when I hear), but sooner or later they will know each other.

Ivan is approaching a deadline in his writing. He feels under pressure and he is uncertain in his relationship with Anna, an uncertainty he does not have time for. On one hand, he has done whatever it was he set out to do and that act, that part of the anatomy, has lost its value. On the other, he does not want to be that man, the one who walks away from a bed, who is so predictable.

Still, that the world diverts him more and she tempts him less creates a movement outward. Even if he will not admit it himself, Anna senses it as an air current around her toes.

She looks for explanations for his waning interest. She categorizes him as an introvert, overworked, hard to read. She pretends to herself that he dislikes the fact that she is still married. She wishes it were comme il faut to use the expression *typical man* in regard to his absent-minded indifference, but she knows that this year gender is in large part a construct.

To excuse Ivan for his waning interest, Jens is forgiven for nothing. He is nothing but hopelessness, their conversations are nothing but emptiness, his hands do nothing but fumble. She is annoyed at him for each and every one of the details of their everyday life. The only things she never criticizes are his trips to Oslo. They cause him such evident delight she dare not make an issue of them.

For Anna, one of the premises of infidelity is its having no future. Its function is not to be enduring but to conclude in some kind of outburst, from which they will be able to move on to the next thing, buoyed by the feeling that something has happened, of being betrayed and tricked out of a promised eternity.

As for many people, the primary function of this dream of forever is to create sorrow afterwards. But Anna cannot articulate this in so many words. She must, instead, give the impression of setting her sights on the long term.

The act of at once pushing for a development neither wants and resisting what they are both pushing for: this is what lends complexity to their intimate moments.

In spite of the discord, Anna and Ivan are in agreement that what they have is important. Ivan is uncertain how it happened, but time has been invested now, the relationship has become part of his interior world, quotidian, somewhat less labour-intensive by dint of its being established.

Anna barely registers, barely consciously, that the love that was supposed to emerge from her baring her soul to a thinker, a love of inner greatness, is surprisingly similar to the thing that wasn't love last time either.

Sometimes it happens that Anna is talkative, full of energy, that she forgets to sweep herself up in enigmatic silence. Often Ivan is too concerned with himself to be in a mood to discuss things. He feels browbeaten at night: Åke has retired and his new editor is Anna's age. There's no harmony between them: she wants him to rewrite, her standard references are different to the ones he usually cites.

When this happens, Anna's words have a tendency to take up too much space, or she is a little too obvious with her tokens of affection, a little too easy. That's how it is: easy to get complacent. She believes that since Ivan claims to be someone who pays no attention to what's on the surface, he will want to see what's inside her, and plenty of it. She gets the idea that since he is interested in his own spiritual life, she is free to ask for his attention.

Anna also likes to stick her nose in Ivan's armpit and put her hand on his soft belly, while he prefers more conventional acts of sensuality, and this tends to make her feel replaceable. She fuels their fights, escalates them, makes moves to end the relationship. All the boredom of getting what you want is burned off when you are unsure whether you can hold on to it. Each time they have mimed their parting, they return to one another, more certain in their knowledge that their feelings can overcome anything.

But all their misunderstandings wear out in the end. All the big fights become small fights. All the last farewells have been made before. Such is the lover's reach; such is the mistress's scope. And yet: so hard to let go of the image of oneself one believes is reflected in the eyes of the other.

*

Anna calls Jens at regular intervals to ask for their account-ant's number or for his tweak to the tarte Tatin recipe or to discuss what they're going to get Hedda as a high school graduation present.

They talk about the same things they talk about in bed and at the breakfast table: how the children are doing and what they should do about how the children are doing.

Anna calls Jens on Wednesday but he is in the middle of something else, he is busy doing something, he does so much these days and hasn't the space to talk.

That Jens has a lot on could be interpreted as a sign that he has met someone too, a *her* to call under cover of darkness. He tends to refer to this person as *going to Oslo* when he talks to Anna, a destination she chooses not to question.

She also chooses not to see Jens's tranquillity for what it is: a sign that he has put the unpleasantness of their last call behind him and no longer allows himself to be pro-voked by trifles. A sign that Oslo is as much a person – a consultant at his company, prepared to wait till he's single, talented winter sportswoman, loves a duet – as it is a real location.

Yet still it (Oslo, she uses Jens's terminology) chafes away at the back of her mind, a presentiment that she will not admit to herself but which has consequences, a presentiment that makes her cling tighter to Ivan.

Anna and Ivan have gone to Signhildsborg, Ivan's home. Anna is going to cook a long-promised dinner for Ivan. Jens is in Oslo, so Anna must secure or repair something with

Ivan, hence the cooking, which is not normally a feature of their relationship.

They walk about the house and he looks at her to see whether she understands the symbolism and weight of the objects in it. Anna makes her face reflect feelings about these things, as though she will one day own them, or hope to. Perhaps such a hope exists. There is a painting in the downstairs hallway that she would like to be able to point at in a nonchalant manner; there is a table about which she would like to say to guests, it doesn't matter if your glasses leave rings.

Anna moves quietly among the papers in Ivan's office, as in a museum. The newspaper profiles are casually filed, undated, in folders, and yet they have been kept, mixed in among scribbled notes that seem to be a treasure trove of Ivan's thoughts.

For a long time, good reviews were to be expected, certainly not something to frame. Now good reviews are a courtesy or a rarity. Ivan tries not to care about it, he tries to find that creative impulse, impervious to reception, not reliant on affirmation, that he believes he felt when he first started writing.

He gestures to the reviews: all that is merely fluff. And yet: folded and refolded, the papers are there. At certain moments, in his darker moods, he cannot keep himself away from them.

The newsprint is dry and unaccommodating, desiccated after just a few years or after all these years. Several of the articles portray Ivan in this same understated office, his gaze piercing the camera's lens. They admit no doubt that the words borne from this gaze are important and must be allowed to emerge by any means necessary. Everything else must fall away. Like the sense of time, like wiping down the kitchen sink. Like using the wrong toothbrush multiple times or leaving shoes in the middle of the doorway – a hindrance, if only a small one, to other people, people he tends to describe, when he writes, as his fellow men.

Anna picks up pieces of paper, one after the other, conscious of being in the room in the picture. She is allowed to look through the drawer where Ivan files drafts, and their expectation is that these notes will prove Ivan's right to her hands, that these drafts will contain something great, something previously hidden, that she will show him she can now see.

But she does not really understand what she is reading. Hopefully it is her own tiredness, but she cannot seem to grasp a single word that makes sense, not a single thought. Nothing is meaningful. The realization is so unpleasant that it must pass immediately.

Wine? Ivan calls from the kitchen. Anna calls him *darling*. She tells him she loves his house. Jens is in Oslo. There is nothing for it but to love Ivan and Ivan's house.

Anna writes to Ivan as usual, she writes about putting the sheets through the mangle and boiling yellow beetroot and serving it with butter in the brown bowl with a green edge and how the thought of him brings her to orgasm.

She writes about the single peony on her bedside table. About impossibly complicated rituals and processes that she knows make him think of times past, of softness in a time unremembered: through her letters she can show herself in the light of a time that no longer exists, or perhaps never existed. Half as real, she is twice as desirable.

She describes her teacup in the evening and how she bakes, how dough rises under linen cloths in a bowl with a cracked rim. She writes that all this has value for her, as though she is the type who lives for the little things. She writes that she wishes he could see her as her hands carry out each action: cutting the meat, slicing the bread, spreading the butter. She makes it sound as though it were she who ate the butter.

She writes that she wants to iron his shirts. She buys shirts – it is not Jens's money, it is their money – and washes them and irons them and then she writes that she wants to unbutton them and run her hands across his neck as he sits there writing. That she longs to be a silent shadow behind him in his house, a scent of bread, the rind of a cheese at the end of the day. *Nothing else is needed*, she writes, *when we are together*.

I need so little, just to sleep in the easy chair in your room, with the sun like a cat at my feet. She writes that she is painting her toenails red and thinking of him. That she thinks of his hands around her ankle. She lets her words describe all the ways she could be silent, if they were together.

He writes that she writes captivatingly; this is a reward.

Anna is going to read her book. It is important to read novels. She turns the pages. Something scrapes at the windowpane. It is the branch of the birch tree as usual. Her hands travel over her body. Her hands are testing: here is the hollow in her pelvis. She can feel it better if she lies on one side, she can grasp it with several fingers. She can feel her ribs here. The feel of her ribs makes her wet. She runs a hand over her hard collarbones, the edges of her kneecaps, feels the air between her fingers as she grasps one wrist with her other hand. Her cheeks flush.

She makes a fist and feels it find space in the gap between her thighs, slides her hand in under her nightdress, in under the edge of her underwear. But then her fingertips stumble against something rough, a trace of hair. She stiffens. Hair, growing here. She switches off the light, shifts to her other side, smooths over her rumpled nightdress, flips the warm pillow and shuts her eyes hard. The birch continues scraping, the wind is picking up.

The end of a relationship has a shape as tangible as that of its beginning.

One of the parties, usually the woman, must give things back, speak harsh words, delete numbers or, if she is younger, social media accounts. She must not be able to understand how this happened!

She must tear at things, fling open doors and turn up at strange addresses. She must sit in a taxi while the male party attempts to bring calm. She must drown him out with her tears and her cries and she must not be receptive to common-sense arguments.

When he sees all these signs of longing for him, he must blaze up in a last pyrotechnic performance, like a fire-eater, like a dancer on coals, which must lead to some kind of touch that will have regained its charge by no longer being taken for granted.

The average couple must tell themselves approximately four to five times that their relatively natural break-up spasms are really signs they were not done with each other after all.

To work this deception on themselves, they must listen to music. Music strengthens feelings and entreats the listener to interpret it as a personal commentary on the events of their own life that the author of the song cannot possibly have intended.

Four to five times they must write that last letter. Key to the composition of the last letter is that it demands an answer: writing a last letter is an invitation.

Four to five times they must allow their fingertips to linger in each other's palms, or slam the car door against the rain, or let the rain fall against the car door as an excuse to sit and watch the anger turn to desire in each other's faces.

If the couple return to each other more than four to five times, one of them has probably had a difficult childhood. These are special cases, marginal. After four to five times even reconciliation is pointless.

Four to five times is what it takes to realize that the great rupture is counterproductive, that it leaves them wanting more and must therefore be administered in increasingly concentrated doses, without ever producing the desired effect. Instead they must learn from children. They must let go of each other as a child lets go of its mother's hand.

Anna is frustrated by Jens's new, evident happiness. She cannot admit this frustration to herself, since the happiness derives from his infidelity, which she does not intend to know about. She channels her annoyance into dissatisfaction with Ivan.

Since Jens has become happy and therefore more attractive, Anna thinks Ivan has become predictable. So Anna is planning to leave Jens, because then she will get Ivan's full attention. She believes his full attention will be more interesting than his partial attention.

Ivan, in turn, is pushing Anna to leave Jens so they can be together, the reason being that she is wearisome. He is tired and distracted, his deadline has passed and reappeared further ahead. He has no time to fill his days with wishing, with longing. He determines that a more established form would make the relationship less demanding, that Anna would take up less of his time if she were part of the furniture.

Now it is settled that Jens must be left, it still remains for Anna and Ivan to settle on when the leaving is to take place. They agree that it must be as soon as possible but can never find the right moment. They both blame this on Anna. Anna claims to be in doubt, so that Ivan will try and convince her. Ivan claims Anna is in doubt to avoid taking responsibility for his own doubts.

Anna considers the possibility that today might be the day it happens, that the decision will happen to her; she thinks this every day. She carries the possibility, carries it inside her. Perhaps today is the day she will leave.

The conversation she will have with Jens plays out in her mind in various forms. It starts in the morning when she wakes up and continues throughout the day. Behind her conversations with colleagues and clients is the soundtrack of her possible statements, his possible replies, until it's as though the scene has already run its course. Behind the light from her desk lamp, the metro carriage, the laundry room is another light, the glow from a door that stands ajar.

Anna steps out of the bath and dries off and sits down at her desk with a cup of tea. After an important meeting with an important lover you must express yourself in writing. Today she has promised she will leave Jens, yet more proof that Ivan is important.

Anna sorts her papers instead of writing on them. Tension passes through her in waves. She feels a sting in her groin and in her hands. She pictures Jens sitting down heavily, maybe running a hand over his eyes. Or he will do something else to indicate shock even more clearly.

She walks in and out of the kitchen. She turns the radio on, she turns it off again. This is not a night for radio, it is a special night, this is the night she will leave, potentially.

123

She puts the eggs in the fridge and she puts the coffee in the cupboard. She puts the oranges in their bowl. They are in season, the blood oranges, though it's coming to an end. You can slice them very thinly, for example, and serve them with walnuts. Juicing them first thing in the morning is also delicious, not unpleasantly sweet like the juice you buy. Though perhaps it eats away at your teeth just as much.

Next week or next month. Anna is certain it will happen this evening. So certain that she has taken out her bag and put things into it, the things she always packs when tonight is the night, the things she always packs when she is certain.

She has spoken to Ivan and they have decided, somewhat wearily, that it has to happen now, just as one decides on a trip no one feels like taking any more, when the weather has changed. He says, You have to stop changing your mind now, and she says, You know I love you but it's hard, and he says something about individual freedom – that is, roughly the same thing as usual, but now in a slightly more resigned tone of voice.

That resigned tone frightens Anna, so she leaves her bag out on the bed, a clear indication of the seriousness of this moment. Whatever happens, Anna thinks, I suppose I really mean this, right?

Anna thinks of how the light will fall into the room and show the darkness under her eyes. She thinks, perhaps I will smoke a cigarette as I speak to Jens. If I lean against the kitchen counter with a glass of wine in my hand and ask: Our agreement, does it even apply any more? Imagine if I say that to Jens, if I blurt it out. There will be no turning back.

The adrenaline rushes from her fingertips to her shoulders and back again. Anna gets four cups out of the dishwasher, two in each hand. She adjusts the wording, testing out the sentences, her voice. She wouldn't take these cups, but maybe the blue ones.

Maybe it's going to happen tonight, maybe Jens will be... something, maybe angry? Maybe he'll finally lose his head and throw me against the wall, or maybe slap me at last so it leaves a mark on my cheek. Maybe he'll beg me to stay? Maybe he'll want to force me. Maybe I'll have to tear myself from his grip, maybe I won't be able to tear myself from his grip. Maybe he'll tear off my clothes. Maybe his pain will make him unaware of what he's doing. Anna's hands are cold with excitement; all her blood has rushed into her major muscle groups.

Anna cooks and eats an omelette made with two eggs, the slightly larger, brown kind of egg, even though on a night such as this it should be impossible to eat. She drinks a glass of wine without leaving lipstick on the rim. She has a napkin on her lap and she does not read while eating. She tastes the flavours in every mouthful, just as she wrote a few months ago that one should do, that this is quality of life.

Anna looks at herself reflected in the window; the light seems less kind this evening. The polo-neck sweater that was soft a moment ago is now itchy across her throat, and she takes it off. Her trousers, she feels them around her hips; she pulls down the zip at the side and steps out of them too. At first the cool is welcome, but then her hair suddenly looks greasy and her legs pale. It is not enough to change her clothes, she must change her skin. She cannot have a conversation with Jens if her hair smells of fried egg, if there is a film on her teeth.

She showers in water that is just warm enough. Just warm enough doesn't dry the skin. She washes her hair, shaves. She dries herself carefully, between the toes too. She smooths one cream into her legs and another over her face. She dries her hair with the blow-dryer after using a product meant to protect the hair from drying out.

Anna stands in front of the mirror. Her engagement and wedding rings are her only jewellery. She pulls her hair back and applies make-up to bring out the shape of her eyes, her eyebrows, her lips, the curve of her cheeks. None of this will be evident when she is finished. Perhaps her eyebrows are a little too dark? She rubs herself out and starts again.

Now she is clean, she will be able to meet Jens. But what does one wear for this kind of conversation? Something soft, something diaphanous? Or something that will enable her to run out if he gets violent? The thought lingers: Jens reaches for a heavy object, I run out. Who would I run to? It's dark outside, I would be weak and fragile and cold, standing on the steps outside someone's house as I rang their doorbell, someone who would see me and protect me from all this. Her face in the mirror glows.

Anna inspects her eyes and finds them to have a certain shine, a shine that says something is going to happen. She sees that her lips are parted, she feels her breath on her lips, she knows what this means. Looking in the mirror is a way to make the time pass, to stop the time passing. The fact that she stays standing there, paralysed, she is taking this moment seriously.

Anna looks in the bathroom mirror. There is nothing else she can do. She cannot do anything constructive about what she sees there, not now. She cannot get out her tweezers and pluck hairs from her eyebrows, she cannot have that kind of calm, that kind of steady hand tonight.

There are many other jobs that need doing but that she cannot start now: painting her nails, pumicing her feet, painting her nails with a second coat of polish. The time should be able to be filled. But tonight it deserves to be made better use of than that, it must be borne in a state of tension.

Anna puts her hands to her cheeks and feels them growing warm, she puts her hands to her chest and feels her heart beating. She sees herself with her hands on her chest, she sees her gaze. Her heart beats faster, it could be arousal. Is this how I would look if I were about to come? thinks Anna. Is this what they would see beneath them?

This is a night for having a second glass of wine. She takes her glass out onto the veranda and she smokes a cigarette and feels the years fall away. She thinks about Jens and how he might be crushed. She wonders if he will hang himself; that would be awful, of course. She thinks of Ivan and how he will hold her face in his hands when they get the news that Jens has died, how her cheeks will be deathly pale.

It is almost half eight before the door slams. Jens clatters about in the fridge and looks up, tired, when she enters the kitchen. He turns back to the eggs and milk. It is obvious he has not seen the shine in her eyes, perhaps the room is too dark.

Can you watch the news first with someone you are about to leave? Anna is burning up inside. Can he see it now, or is he dazzled by the light of the screen?

Can the news be on in the background as you do it, as you are leaving someone? If you happen to start watching the news together, can you interrupt it to leave them? Anna and Jens watch the news. Do we even exist any more? The words burn in her throat but are impossible to say while the TV is on.

And afterwards, after the news? They brush their teeth. You cannot say anything while brushing your teeth, it's physically impossible.

The bag on the bed, does it require comment now they have come into the bedroom? Is it obvious what kind of bag it is? Anna can feel her heart in her throat: it's going to happen now, everything is going to be split open and I'll be someone else from this point on.

But no, Jens doesn't notice the bag. He unbuttons his shirt and he unbuttons his trousers and Anna sees the glow of the street lamp on his stomach and you cannot say all those things she has planned out about her feeling of time passing, about marking time, to someone who has no clothes on.

Anna draws the curtains. Anna remarks that the apple tree needs pruning again and Jens agrees. Should we pasteurize the juice this summer… though I guess we may as well just freeze it, Anna says, and Jens says that sounds fine.

The birch blows against the ceiling, rain blows against the ceiling. Anna closes her eyes and listens to Jens's breathing. She thinks white laundry in the breeze, white laundry in the breeze, but the thought does not calm her, the words are on their way up out of her throat. She tries to breathe. She thinks of a funeral, her own or someone else's, the shoes she wore would depend on whose it was. She thinks of strangulation marks around her throat and of hiding them beneath a new scarf.

Jens, says Anna in the darkness, I have.

You have what? Jens says.

Nothing, don't worry, Anna says, I was just wondering if I'd locked up, darling.

You always lock up, Jens says.

PART THREE

For most people, life involves a number of crisis-like events in which we come close, close, close to allowing our inner selves to manifest. But for the majority, these moments give us nothing more than a sense of clear-sightedness, an opportunity to congratulate ourselves on our insight, without consequences.

From a purely narrative point of view, there should be a turning point here, a juncture where it becomes impossible for everything to go on as usual, where the awareness of what 'as usual' is becomes too heavy and something snaps. There should be space in fiction to learn something, to develop.

But life is not like that. Life does not offer up teachable moments. Of course you notice things about yourself and those close to you, of course you realize things. But then you turn away.

The rules carry so much more weight than emotional honesty does. Against the rules, will is no more than a sigh, as insipid as a sigh, as toothless. One of these rules is that when someone is dying, or has an illness wasting their body, or has aged to the point of helplessness, it is *the woman's role to provide care. The course of events can vary in rhythm and intensity, from the long months of late-stage metastasis to the long years of degenerative illness. Regardless, the illness must inflect every aspect of life. The woman's life must be subsumed into the life that is nearing its end.*

When the separation finally does occur, it is relatively uncomplicated. Uncomplicated in the sense of being predictable. It is Jens who leaves, and he does it in a way Anna finds sudden, unplanned.

A few days after Jens's final departure for Oslo – days of very little dialogue, during which Anna feels silenced despite countless calls to her children, calls spent crying, calls she ends by hanging up suddenly to make them call her back – Anna too packs the objects she will take to Signhildsborg and her new life.

Anna packs quickly, almost giving the impression that she's leaving a house someone is about to come home to and ask her to stay in.

Anna packs as though she has not packed and unpacked her bag many times before, for the same sole reason each time. She packs as though all her doubts were unfounded.

She packs as though leaving were as easy as this simple act, as though the actual divorce were a matter of emotion, not practicality. As though she would not have to walk in and out of the front door again countless times and still be familiar with the smell in the hall, that blend of floor polish and natural materials, before everything is sold or divided up between the children's new apartments.

As though Anna would never again need to think about whether she should cut the grass or remind Jens to cut the grass. As though the grass stops growing between the point a person leaves and the point the house is sold.

Anna wishes she had only to pack symbolic objects, but she must also keep in mind the everyday ones. Charger, tooth-brush, tablets. Her bag is on the bed, like in a film. One must have scarves in my situation, she thinks, getting them out.

If the children had been younger she would have packed their drawings with tears running down her cheeks, or if it had been another time, framed photographs. But none of that needs packing. The children no longer draw, she has the photos on her phone. She feels it anyway, a sense of having forgotten something.

My place is with Ivan now, she thinks. There is no alternative, and so it must be a great love. All the way to Signhildsborg, even that last stretch along the unmade road and up the drive, she is full of this great new thing, being separated, separated because of her love for Ivan, she tells herself.

She imagines a film camera panning out as she parks, from the close-up of her face to a wider angle that cap-tures both her movements and the poplars in the wind, the peonies by the front door that have passed their prime but not been cut back, as if they were waiting for her hand. The door slams as they stand in the hallway, closed by the same wind that was tearing at the poplars.

*

The first month at Signhildsborg is bright. It is a Tuesday and Ivan is out and Anna is standing in the kitchen thinking that this is the best time for tomatoes. She thinks it would be nice to have a tomato salad for dinner. She is drying her hands on a tea towel when Ivan returns from his business in town and comes into the kitchen, something she has already realized is an unusual thing for men of his generation to do outside of mealtimes.

Anna can see something has happened and assumes it is connected to his book: she recalls him telling her he was visiting his publisher – this editor and the problems she creates, thinks Anna – but Ivan has come to tell her he is dying.

I'm dying, he says, and starts to cry.

When they have regained some level of composure, the statement is elucidated. For a long time, Ivan has had pains around his ribcage, something he interpreted as stress over the book. Now he has finally, and against his principles, sought medical advice. He has after several visits been diagnosed with an aggressive form of cancer, which in its present advanced state is impossible to treat.

While she holds him, Anna orients her thoughts along appropriate lines: she does *not* think about the fact that he did not tell her he was going to the hospital. She does *not* think that he must have been there several times before getting this diagnosis. She does *not* think, When he first felt those pains he didn't tell me and when he saw a doctor he didn't tell me, and when he waited for the results and the new tests and the new results, he didn't tell me.

She does *not* think about who he might have told instead, who he has turned to while not turning to her. She does *not* think about coincidences or replaceability or chance.

She puts his silence down to the fact he is a man. Such a typical man, she thinks, this time without trying to restrain her stereotyping. Then she moves on. She tells herself she is his next of kin.

Anna is the next of kin. She has a job, a task: caring for Ivan in his last days. When her surprise has settled and Ivan has accepted the situation, a calm descends on the house. The autumn is still full of possibilities. Ivan's impending death is so abstract it acts almost as the flattering backdrop to a series of events to which it lends greater gravity. Everyone knows what they must do.

He must finish writing his book, it is urgent. Because it will be his last it is assumed to be better than recent ones, if not quite better than all his earlier books. The editor and beleaguered publisher are more cheerful, with an eye to the posthumous reviews.

Anna thinks how lucky it is that she is here now, to guard the space required to write a masterpiece.

Ivan must also bid farewell to friends and acquaintances. Anna writes lists of dishes and plans baking sessions: they must not arrive to an empty table when they have come to say goodbye, but neither should they be allowed to intrude upon the creative process.

Anna must arrange things: for the funeral, for a possible donation to the library, for a possible sale of his art, depending on how much it is deemed to be worth. Anna buys a bound notebook. Ivan sits in his office and calls out to her sometimes. She enters the new needs in her book.

Anna dresses practically, in woollen sweaters and durable trousers. They take walks when Ivan has enough strength, and it is a lovely autumn, undebatable now, one of the loveliest in a long time.

Ivan does not grow noticeably sicker, not then, in those first weeks. Death hangs there like a working title, not troubling them with its presence. Sometimes he does not care for the seasoning of a dish. Sometimes he is a little tired, but it is nothing that cannot be solved by taking a rest on the sofa in his office, under the soft grey blanket.

After a month there is a change for the worse. Ivan's daughter, Siri, comes to visit. This upsets the balance of the household.

What even are you to him, Anna? Siri does not ask, but her raised eyebrows do say, *You must have an abnormally well-developed caring and cleaning gene, Anna, to be getting something out of this.* She also does not say, *What are you getting out of this? It isn't like you've had a life together.* But Anna is not deaf, she hears it all the same.

However, Siri has her own life to live, and after that first weekend she leaves. She has her own life to live, says Ivan, though Anna can't make out what it consists of. Siri has no husband. She has no children. She must be returning to something else, thinks Anna, to something that is not a husband and children but is still more important than Ivan.

When she is stripping the sheets on Siri's bed, and several hours later, when she is hanging them to dry, she ponders this: what Siri's life consists of and what in it could be so important. A life where no one calls out to her? Where she can choose at will which room to be in? Anna puts the sheets through the mangle with three tea towels and the cloth from the table on the glazed veranda.

Anna probes Siri's life, the thought of one after Ivan. A room. In the room, a chair? An invisible room, an invisible woman in the chair, an invisible shoulder without anyone's hand on it, dinners chewed consisting of what? Anna shakes off Siri's life: Ivan is not dead yet; they still go to private views sometimes, sometimes even to small dinners.

Nothing is said about when Siri will return; they reassume their routines. Ivan sits in his office and Anna moves about the house, arranging the vases, buying the cheeses.

Anna asks Ivan whether Siri has ever wanted children, or if something happened. Ivan says he never asked, has never considered the question. I believe people differ when it comes to those things, he says. He pushes his cup away with a grimace. The tea has been steeping too long, it's not really hot.

Ivan's impending death brings admin, delegated to Anna in her capacity as someone who can still make sense of forms. Apart from this she carries out many tasks resembling those one must carry out with a child. Getting through the day has once again become the day's main content. But the lifting has got harder. A fully grown man weighs more than a recalcitrant child.

Anna is the one who puts the coffee cups in the dishwasher, scrubs the milk off the pans, sweeps the crumbs off the floor and puts yesterday's papers in the recycling. She is the one who takes the empty jars to the bottle bank and changes the toilet roll and nips brown leaves off the pelargonium so she and Ivan will not have to live these last days in squalor. She adapts their food to his appetite and excuses Ivan's behaviour towards those around him, who are fortunately understanding since they are not forced to live with him round the clock.

Anna is the one who thumps the vacuum cleaner against the threshold of the dying man's office and the one who puts his jacket back on its hanger and picks up the blanket from the floor and tidies the ash in the grate and calls the glazier and the roofer and the plumber and indicates with her hands the cracks and blockages that still need seeing to, despite all the death.

Anna is the one who shoves the lawnmower through even the thick, mossy patches in late autumn and then the snow shovel through the gravelly patches in the middle of winter and who queues at the supermarket and lines up the items on the conveyor belt and pays for the food and boils the water despite the dying man's lack of appetite. She is the one who eats in silence if it is that kind of day.

There is no cleaner at Signhildsborg. Anna discovers this absence as she scrubs and vacuums.

Not having a cleaner for political reasons and not having one for financial reasons produces the same result: dirt. There is no point in analysing Ivan's reasons for not having a cleaner; the dirt is there regardless. Anna takes a constructive approach. She scours.

Money is not something Anna and Ivan talk about; the absence of a cleaner is not mentioned. She stands there with a toothbrush and gets into the spaces between the tiles.

It goes on being autumn, as it usually does for several months of the year. Ivan is doing worse. Siri comes to visit again and apparently sees something that makes her return the very next weekend: some sign, or perhaps they have had a conversation.

Can't we just buy bread, says Siri on her way through the kitchen. She never stops in the kitchen except at mealtimes or occasionally to rest her hip against the kitchen counter and eat a piece of fruit. She reaches out a hand to the fruit bowl, expecting to find it full. She might eat three apples, as long as they're Swedish, and throw the cores in the sink; she might eat a pear and lean over the counter so the juice drips and leaves sticky marks.

Someone about to bury a parent ranks higher than someone about to bury a lover after a relatively short relationship. Higher value is placed on Siri's feelings than on Anna's. Siri is not afraid to play this trump card. It means she has to be allowed to talk on the phone even though Ivan has just fallen asleep and it might be nice to have a moment of peace.

Siri can slope off to do yoga and collect herself. Siri has to be allowed to feel that she can meet other people, get some air, she has to be allowed to take care of herself. She uses those words, as though she had a right to them by dint of being herself, that she *has to be allowed*.

She does other things without talking about it. She moves about as though it were natural for her to leave her breakfast mug on the table – this is her childhood home, after all – and to put only the one sweater she brought with her into the washing machine, even though there are two tea towels and a pillowcase in the laundry basket.

It's easy to revert to being a child in the company of your parents, Anna thinks. Because she is about to become fatherless, Siri has reverted to childhood, thinks Anna, she is like a child. She thinks this again and again, the same words: like a child, like a child, like a child. Sometimes she thinks: like a man, like a man, like a man.

AGNES LIDBECK

Then Anna corrects herself: it can't be easy for Siri. It can't be easy to be thirty-eight and alone, almost forty, it can't be easy, she thinks, hanging Siri's skirts, a larger size than her own, on the line. They cannot be put through the mangle, so she irons them; Siri does not notice that her skirts have been ironed, her underwear folded and left neatly on the edge of the bed when she comes in. She just puts them on again, the next time, as though they were the inexhaustible fruit in the bowl.

Anna says to Siri that it must be exciting to travel as much as she does for work. She says it as a question but gets no response, Siri sees nothing to respond to. When Anna speaks to her, Siri knows that everything Anna asks has been answered by someone else long ago.

Siri walks around Signhildsborg with a sense of ownership towards its objects, but also a sense of ownership towards its very centre, towards Ivan. She alternates between acting tenderly towards him and being angry at him; they allow her both these feelings, she and Ivan.

Siri walks through the rooms gathering small objects of significance by which to remember her father and her life up to his death. She packs them as though she is never coming back here.

As if there are not going to be weeks, months of conversations about which butter knives are made of silver and which can be thrown out and about curtains that need taking down, of meetings with the estate agent at the kitchen table and painting over the place on the back of the bathroom door where Siri's mother marked their heights.

As if death did not have clear commonalities with divorce in having, ultimately, more practical consequences than emotional ones.

Failing to see things in the other that they would rather not see in themselves is not a lack of imagination. It is the definition of empathy.

Refraining from seeing through someone is not short-sighted. It is a kindness that borders on compassion. The closest you can come to true understanding is closing your eyes to each other's minutiae.

That is why the person providing care must always overlook, must look away from, the shortcomings of the person who is sick.

The carer must not wish the time away. Neither must they be irritated by life's triteness.

The carer's experience of the moment must be as though she had read about it in a glossy magazine, even if the particulars as they are actually lived are the same as they were previously: tidying rooms, filling in personal details, cleaning, cooking, smiling.

Ivan's illness eats away at his body, of course; that is why its name is cancer, because it has claws. But he also grows even less keen on intellectual conflict than before. He is no longer looking for bite, he has lost the stamina to try and win. Only a peevish dissatisfaction remains, like kicking at a sticky door that refuses you that satisfying slam.

As he has become impotent – a combination of low-level depression, poor nutrient absorption and the side effects of all his medicines – he has also lost the need for a sexual object.

Instead, his claim to Anna's body is equal to a child's. It is important that she can carry a shopping bag, keep to a list and take a temperature. Fellatio, on the other hand, is no longer a necessary skill.

Anna and Ivan still cannot acknowledge this shift in function. Ivan must continue, technically, to be a man, in the same way he is, technically, writing, and is, in theory, engaged in public life.

Anna bends forward, in her back a softness that indicates she is not thinking of how she will subsequently, at another stage, straighten it. Anna pretends to ignore the powerlessness implied by the fact that Ivan can only wear socks, that his feet have swollen too much for shoes.

As she purees his food she continues to relate to Ivan as to a living man with a claim to her breathing. As though the man there in the chair were still a lover who could get up and grasp her waist and bend her backwards and say *Ah, you can do the dishes later.*

Siri has a lot to do. Many of the things she does are things Anna views as her jobs, which means Anna has to find other things to do, the things left over, so as not to be redundant. The leftover tasks are always the most basic ones, such as cleaning tea leaves out of the sink, scrubbing couscous off the bottom of the pan, or putting the pan in to soak so as to be able to scrub off the couscous later.

Siri does not bathe Ivan, that would be hard for a daughter, but she does talk to him. She plays Ivan records, the ones he used to play to Anna when they first met. Siri does not do the nights with Ivan. That would be odd, that is Anna's place, says Siri, it's not like I can take your place, she says, indicating the roomy armchair set at an angle to Ivan's bed.

Some evenings Siri wants to sit in that chair and talk to Ivan, but the next evening she absolutely does not want to. So Anna has to tell Ivan it's just her putting him to bed this evening, because Siri is feeling sad. Anna is lying; Siri is not particularly sad. Anna happens to know that Siri is sitting with her cigarettes and a book, but she's not about to say that, though she thinks she could; she could say,

pointedly, *No, Siri appears to have other plans this evening.*
But you can't upset someone who is dying.

However: Siri often talks to Ivan in the evenings. It is
important to her, she says. On Friday evenings she reads
The Man Without Qualities at his bedside. Siri reads poems
and sings songs. She reads the Bible to Ivan. She plays his
guitar and dances in front of him to Leonard Cohen, slowly
waltzing round to the music.

She hangs new paintings in Ivan's room on the ground
floor because she knows these are the ones he has always
liked best. She rests photos that have lain packed in boxes
against the bookshelves. She points out of the window and
says, Listen, what kind of bird do you think that is?

Siri talks to Ivan about memories: Do you remember when we played chess, when we went skating, do
you remember that time in London? She asks Ivan if he
remembers and Ivan nods or blinks or smiles or mumbles
something, depending on how long it is since Anna gave
him his evening medication.

Then Siri leaves again and is gone for a week or so and
when that happens it must be remembered that her life
cannot simply stop. Next Friday evening she comes back
and walks straight over to Ivan and Ivan lights up and lets
go of Anna's hand.

After lunch Siri combs the bookshelves and takes out the
books worth keeping. But she ends up just standing there,
daunted by the metres of shelves left over, the books without dedications or provenance.

Siri calls her mother to ask her advice on how these and

other essential matters ought to be dealt with, the things that have to do with the soul and/or value of the house and the many things in it.

Anna walks through the same rooms as Siri a little later. The objects Siri snatches up and moves around spread a lot of dust, and Anna trails her with a vacuum cleaner while Siri weighs things in her hands.

Anna calls the carpenter to ask why he did not come to fix the warped door at the appointed time. She calls the hospital to enquire about the colour of Ivan's vomit.

It will not be easy to clear Signhildsborg, but Siri is resolved to sell, even though it is so clearly a place to stay in. This decision has been made in spite of the fact that Ivan is still alive, but has not been communicated to him as it could cause upset. Ivan sometimes talks vaguely of a museum, a cultural centre.

The house is full of carefully preserved things, or things that have been put down and now seem immovable. A pair of child's shoes with perished rubber soles on the windowsill, the distance between a chair and table that is perfectly suited to someone else's height.

On the chest of drawers in what was, for the first part of autumn, Anna and Ivan's bedroom, and before that Siri's mother and Ivan's bedroom, but which is now just an empty room with a few folded pairs of trousers draped over the back of a chair, there is a brass candelabra so crooked it would be a fire hazard to light a candle in it. Nonetheless it stands there; no one knows how long it has been there and no one would ever ask.

Who would not want to be as constant as a home granted careful consideration? Who would not want to be worn into a floor or forgotten by the window in that same way until one becomes a natural part of the room that no one can force out?

Anna puts a moving box in the old servant's room and in it she puts her own things to stop them getting mixed up with Siri's rational piles: scrap, save, sell. Ivan sleeps in the office now and Anna sleeps in the old servant's room so as to be on hand, or, on bad nights, in the chair beside his bed. She can glimpse the end like a door one might open as spring approaches. What is waiting on the other side is uncertain, for both parties.

Anna and Siri go about in silence. Siri is sorting Ivan's private papers and photos. Anna is wiping down the counters again. Siri brings out one of the boxes full of photos of Ivan and Siri and her mother, photos Ivan took of Siri and the adults took of each other. It's the seventies and eighties. How gorgeous she was, she says. Look how thin she was too. Anna looks at the photos closely. Siri's mother really was very thin.

Anna's jobs are clearly delineated but not completely uncomplicated. They have to be planned with a degree of concentration. But still. Still they leave space, in the back of her mind, for thoughts of afterwards. She thinks of Ivan, or his good sides: it is an exercise in remembering him. But thinking about Ivan does not fill the whole day. There are gaps.

While Anna is ironing, she makes a mental tally of the women she knows who live without men, post-men. She recalls their names, inextricably alike, their faces, inextricably alike, their days, intangible, their travel, inconsequential. She remembers a woman she had read about who had no one to unbutton the back of her dress at bedtime. Anna feels a knot in her stomach and calls her children; her children confirm she has a name: Mamma, Mamma, I don't have time right now.

Before society reached its current level of secularization, people routinely sought forgiveness on their deathbed. It was presumed that the dying would confess their sins to a priest, who would act as an interpreter for a god who would, in turn, absolve their sins.

Today people are simply expected to forgive one another without recourse to a higher authority. This raises a number of questions.

Is it up to the carer to determine what is and is not forgivable? Should she take it for granted that all is forgiven? Or should she avoid such demarcations?

Should she make it easy to forgive by hiding those last confessions behind tubes in the throat and morphine in the blood, by putting beeping monitors in the corner and installing humming fluorescent lights on the ceiling?

And, in the event that any words should still find their way through, something that rings true, should these words be blamed on the pain or confusion of the dying individual? Should those words that are spoken towards the end be inaudible, inaudible enough to echo in the mind later, to fill the memory with something to be interpreted?

Today it is Tuesday, February. The time is eight o'clock; it is growing light. Ivan sits at his computer in the office.

The fact that Ivan is sitting at his desk is a kind of grandstanding one can forgive or not forgive. In any case, he is the very image of the working man. Sitting in the office in lieu of actually writing.

Because he is sitting in his office he fulfils the part of his task that consists of being the one who has something to write, the one who is capable of writing this something, and thus he is Ivan and therefore worthy, worth Anna's attentions. That she is caring not for just any old man but for a man of a certain stature. He is in his place of work, therefore he is working. The sentences above are not what Anna thinks. Anna's thoughts do not venture beyond the fact that she helped Ivan to his office at 5 a.m., and that he has therefore been working for three hours and breakfast will soon be ready. Tea in the pot, bread on the board, a little blue floral plate with his eight o'clock tablets.

Siri comes in through the door from the hall. Her hair is strongly scented and Anna notices that it is still a little damp above her forehead. Siri takes her usual seat.

Anna goes to help Ivan, supporting him as he walks to his chair. Anna does not think Siri is behaving as though she were at a hotel – that would be ungracious. Instead she thinks: I have forgotten the honey.

Ivan and Siri discuss Ivan's book. Anna reminds herself to lay a hand on his elbow to remind him to take his medication.

Ivan's argument is incomprehensible, influenced by the morphine and by trying to figure out his own thoughts. It's like a conversation, Ivan says, a dialogue back through epochs of myself. Anna stirs the contents of the teapot. A conversation, a dialogue, a tonality, Ivan continues, raising an eyebrow as Anna cuts cheese while he is mid-sentence. He breaks off, she stops cutting, one slice is just fine.

Anna turns her eyes on Ivan so he can once again fix Siri with his. The newspapers are on the table, still folded. Ivan starts again, he says *like a conversation* once again but loses his thread. The fact that Anna had not completely forgotten the cheese, that she was still cutting the cheese, was evidently enough to undo him: he is silent now, no words come.

Ivan peers into his teacup and looks thoughtful. Anna peers into hers, not daring to meet Siri's accusatory gaze, unable to swallow her toast, unable to open the newspaper: the rustling would sound like a forest fire now, Anna thinks.

Siri steps in. She glances resolutely through the paper. Anyway, she says, not a single one of the critics is serious these days, right, Pappa, and then she drops the arts and culture section into the butter dish. It's just trash, trash and more trash. Anna picks up the paper and wipes the greasy corner with a kitchen towel. Anything in particular? she asks, her voice neutral, but she gets no response. Ivan looks out at the watery early sunlight between the naked trees; he is still upset about the cheese.

Siri goes on. It's just pointless, she says, just hopeless, trying to have a conversation in this country. It's all just cut-price solutions, everything that gets published is for kids. No one comes anywhere close to the gravity of your writing any more, except for Lars, maybe, and to be quite frank he's started getting repetitive. Tomas maybe, but even he feels pretty mannered.

Ivan turns back to the room, a reward for Siri. He lights up, a little like the tree trunks in the sun, Anna thinks. That's damn true, Siri, he says. His medication has loosened many of the restraints he once placed on himself, the ones that kept his insults free of curse words, for instance. Every time I go up to my publisher's these days, he says, it's just a load of kids. Girls, bloody good-looking girls, they dress like whores, sure, but since when have bloody good-looking girls known anything about politics? Huh? About art? At this, he flaps a hand at the paper. Nothing! Nothing!

Dinner. Siri looks for her special cup and says to no one in particular, Ugh, the dishwasher's full! That can't be directed at me, Anna thinks, since she is on her way out to the car, evidently not on her way to empty the dishwasher.

Since Siri is home, Anna may as well take the opportunity to run a few errands. Not that it would be impossible to leave Ivan on his own for a while, good lord, that wouldn't kill him, but still. It is best to use this moment, since today is not the deadline for that goji berry project at work.

First she drives over to the big supermarket in a concrete box on an industrial estate on the outskirts of the little town, the little town which is really very nice in the summer. She pushes the trolley along the aisles and buys what little they need: Ivan does not eat much these days. They only really need eggs.

But he might conceivably say, in the middle of dinner, that it might be nice to have something extra since Siri's here. I could probably find the time to bake some bread and make a fish soup, Anna thinks. We probably need milk too. And you can never have too much coffee in the house. We could probably make a nice fish soup this evening, one with mussels still in their shells.

Anna wonders if it is sufficiently obvious that she is different to the other people here: that she's a fish out of water. If someone were to get closer, she thinks, they would see a difference in my clothes, note a different scent about me. But would they see that I am suffering more than they are? Would they see that I am bearing a heavier load?

She stops in the middle of the vegetable section, where she catches sight of her face in the mirrors above the produce. The other people are walking about as usual, they do not appear to be suffering particularly, or if they are, the suffering is ugly, like poverty. That is, if there really is poverty in Sweden these days. Bad taste, that does exist, Anna thinks, and obesity. That means something, that kind of loose fat; of course you feel sorry for them, but how hard can it be.

Can they see how tired I am, Anna wonders, meeting her own gaze. Do they want to save me, when they see that? Anna scoops some nuts into a bag. Sometimes you just have to treat yourself.

The carer must put the observer in mind of certain great works of art, the creators of which are generally seen to possess greater genius than their models. What all great works of art have in common is the fact they exist to elicit pleasure in the observer.

We like to see the evening sun fall upon the cheek of the portrait's subject because it creates interesting light and shadow on her cheek, not because it warms her.

It is the same with the carer. When words such as strong, patient and empathetic are used to describe her, they should be used as synonyms for self-annihilation.

Anna goes to the pharmacy to collect Ivan's pills. She takes a ticket and marks the importance of her errand by sitting down on one of the green-upholstered chairs and closing her eyes, instead of looking at the vitamin supplements and pumice stones as if it were an ordinary visit.

Those who are collecting morphine-based prescriptions and other items associated with late-stage cancer cannot possibly be interested in manicures or allergies, says her hand as she brings it to her brow, as though every sound were too loud. She waits her turn patiently. Everyone there can see that for her this is a moment of calm, a little distance, just being allowed to sit like this. It must be obvious to everyone that I'm struggling so much that the pharmacy queue has become a relief. I imagine they must be curious, Anna thinks.

After the pharmacy Anna goes to the off-licence. Things are now at the stage where it can hardly make a difference. Ivan drinks a small dram of whisky every evening, not because he enjoys the taste much nowadays but more because the doctor outright forbade it. Anna drinks wine. I have no intention of counting the glasses, she thinks, not when things are the way they are, not when my life is as it is.

There is a cafe next to the off-licence. It is really a very unremarkable cafe, relatively ugly but not very ugly, and their cakes appear to be relatively dull but not very dull. Sitting in a cafe is not the same as sitting in a waiting room, or other things only melancholy people do. It could be conceived, if someone saw her there, that she did not realize it was not enjoyable. They might think she liked lattes or that she liked carrot cake.

What she can do is go in and buy a cup of black coffee to take away, to burn herself on, to drop because of all the bags she's lugging, and to show, as she almost collapses over the spilled cup, how very soon she will be at her limit. She imagines that man with the beard wondering if she is going to faint. She imagines that he cannot help thinking her face is ethereal, almost transparent in the light, that he cannot avoid feeling, through his sympathy with her, a strong sense of attraction.

Or she can buy a cup of black coffee, sink into a chair by the window and stare through it, unseeing. Then the man with the beard might contemplate her neck. She could show that she is so tired she fails to even recognize those of Ivan's acquaintances who pass by outside: the neighbour, the woman from the counter at the hospital, the man who runs the only bookshop. So tired I cannot even wave at them, that's how tired I am. They must understand.

She cannot decide what to do at the cafe, so instead she walks on to the park, a window of openness and light between the buildings. Anna remains there a long time:

without her phone in her hand or a coffee cup. She cannot manage anything else any more, she decides in the chill air. The tears well up in her eyes, the world shudders, and the window is a window to climb through, deceptively like a door.

Anna does not move from the park bench. The bags crowd around her feet, the chill takes up residence in her legs. She must get to the car, she must make dinner. And then? That is a dangerous question to ask: it leads to others.

Anna tries to engage herself in a long list of commitments, a long list of things that take up her time. He must be bathed and read to and his teeth must be brushed, he must be comforted in the night and I must change the sheets on his bed.

There is more to add to the list. Bleach again, for instance. That smell in the second toilet is still there. Work too, of course, that has to stay on the list, because who would she be otherwise? My life is not all about vacuum cleaner bags, Anna thinks, I care deeply about my work.

She is on safe ground for a while with the vacuum cleaner. She thinks, I'll vacuum first, then it will be done, or first I'll make some dough, then I'll vacuum, then bake the bread, then make the soup.

But after the soup there is a precipice. The list comes to an end; the only things that can still be added to it are things she does not normally allow herself to think about, definitely not in concrete terms. But suddenly she is thinking about them anyway, with growing vertigo and a salty taste in her mouth, about how everything will be later, when she will be able to go to the cinema and do all the things she cannot handle right now, when she herself will be responsible for filling a list with things she is not forced into doing.

When Ivan is dead, that is, and she is not. She wonders, even though she is not allowed to, what she will do with herself then, not to mention the other stuff: what dinners will she be invited to, by whom, who will be there to invite her? She is going to be a single woman; who will find her sufficiently interesting to invite to dinner? There is a flash in her peripheral vision. It is the rage, coming at last: there, in the park, Anna gets angry at life.

Of course Anna's breathing speeds up, of course she has to stand – we need not trouble ourselves now with these obvious signs of strong emotion. Faces, words, movements from her memory flicker into view, even though her eyes are open. The children's arms, holding tight, flicker through her mind, and the time she clenched her jaw so hard she broke a tooth. All the times Jens turned away in his sleep, joined into a single movement. All those words she has written and crossed out again. The way her voice has grown gentle.

The park looks different behind this flicker of images, more loaded, as though it were something to write about: the sky and the trees take on new proportions, certain objects glow as she has seen her own cheeks do when they are lit to their best advantage.

When a diagnosis is first confirmed or an accident takes place, there is a great rush of feelings. But it settles, as feelings do; a rush of feelings cannot be constant or even particularly prolonged.

Caring is a time filled with almost-ending. Instead of the final conversation it is a long line of conversations that should be meaningful but are not.

And yet the carer must continue to show interest.

The thought, registered on an intellectual level, that she has been angry and afraid, is easy enough to do away with on the journey home. She plays Erik Satie. The event itself remains in her gut somewhat longer, like an emotion, or perhaps too little lunch, but a glass of wine helps and the final traces are swept away once the fire starts crackling in the stove.

Bedtime comes, then night. Anna sleeps in short bursts, with the usual interruptions for comforting and medicating.

Morning comes and Anna calls Hedda before she starts work and Hedda says nothing in particular. In the separation, Hedda took Jens's side very decidedly, Anna always thinks, wondering why and telling herself that's how it tends to be with girls and their fathers. Anna calls Harry, but it goes to voicemail; she supposes he is working already. Anna always says to herself that Harry is a real rock, so supportive through the separation, as it tends to be with boys and their mothers, she thinks.

Anna remembers that the handle on the fridge door is a little sticky, so she cleans it and then cleans the rest of the fridge. It's odd how dirty it gets, even though she is the only one who gets things in and out. It's not like when the children were little and you expected their fingerprints to be everywhere. I keep my hands clean, thinks Anna, where do these marks come from, these splashes of what?

When she stands up she notices that the top of the fan over the stove is also greasy, so she rinses out the cloth and wipes the fan too. When the alarm tells her it is ten o'clock, Anna gets up from her computer, where she has managed to write *Time to try new—*. Pills again, they cannot be delayed, something tells her. It is important to write in the logbook that they have been taken on the hour.

Ivan has a somewhat unpleasant smell, even though she washes his clothing regularly. It is impossible to avoid, not when she comes so close with the pills in the palm of her outstretched hand, feeling the trust, she assumes it must be trust, that means he never asks if they are the right ones. She does not think: It shows how important I am to him, that he lets me come so close. She cannot stop herself feeling it, the little shiver of power in the hand that is so soft, soft enough to rest his cheek upon, as though he were a baby trusting so much in others' hands that it allows its neck to rest against them.

Ivan blows dust off the computer's keys. Anna plucks a few stray petals from the desk and notices that the bin is almost full, so she takes it away to empty it. With the bin in one hand, she uses the other to pick up two glasses with straws in them.

There's nothing magical about writing, Ivan used to say; the secret is thinking. Thinking the right thoughts: the ones that turn small thoughts into great ones. So why don't you just write? Anna does not ask. What are you thinking about? is another thing she no longer asks, not since he completely gave up pretending to be thinking about her.

Among the thoughts Anna does not think is that Ivan is hiding, that the book is a shield. As long as he is in his office he has no need to face Anna, who is circling out there with her little life in her little soul, as he said the other day. But you must not take such comments personally, she tells herself, it must be his illness. It must be all this death that is making it so hard for him to work, right? It must be his proximity to death that is distracting him and feeding this anxiety that nothing really turns out right, not as right as it ought to be when you are dying.

It is his illness that has taken his appetite from him and his energy and words and patience and it is his illness that makes him so short with her and stops him meeting her gaze or laying his hand on hers when she lays her hand on his. He never asks her to touch him; it must be his illness. He never asks her to say anything; it must be his illness. He asks her to leave him in peace; it must be his illness. It must be something other than himself that makes his gaze pass over her, that makes him call her sympathy smothering, her view of the world naive, her aesthetic trite, her napkins bourgeois and her telephone conversations idiotic.

If he were not about to die, he would not have said that in hindsight it was a mistake to bring her here, to take her out of her own habitat, that she cannot fully understand what it means to live with a creative person. That she should have stayed with Jens, that the whole business had been a mistake. He would not say that were it not for his illness.

If he were not ill, he would not say this: Woman, can't you see you're disturbing me. Anna does not answer. When Ivan's aggression reaches a certain point, it is as though all his words are spoken in a foreign language. She hears from his tone that he is irritated, but she has not the wherewithal to take in its meaning.

Anna goes out, out into the kitchen again and puts the dirty glasses in the sink, but it looks bad so she washes them up. She empties the bin and leaves it in the hallway so as not to disturb him again.

If Ivan were not dying they would be happy together. Then it wouldn't have been a mistake to leave Jens, she thinks, without thinking about the chronology, about who left whom. Because Ivan is going to die, this cannot be a mistake, it must be a great love. Only great emotions, shaded in the ways literature has documented them, are allowed in such proximity to death.

Anna does not think, absolutely not, that Ivan is longing for death just as much as she is afraid of how things will be when he has died. For Anna, Ivan's deathbed is one to be made up, something definite to be taken in hand. Ivan's impending death gives her somewhere to be. What will happen afterwards fills her with worry.

For Ivan, on the other hand, afterwards will bring clarity. Being dead is the most dignified alternative, an excellent excuse for not writing as well as one once had, or not finishing what one is writing, or not writing at all. Death will come like a thick, black, liberating line over the humiliating vagueness of recent years. The recently deceased cannot be reviewed in any other way than with standing ovations. But, as stated, Anna does not think this.

Anna puts away the laptop; it is not nice to have it out in the kitchen. She wipes the lampshade and starts getting lunch ready. Anna slices red cabbage very thinly. She never tires of the pattern inside. She is going to pour some vinaigrette into the salad bowl, she is going to roast a few walnuts. The light falls across the gateleg table and the knife cuts cleanly.

Siri is leaning against the kitchen counter: for once she is in the kitchen. She must be having difficulty concentrating, thinks Anna. Siri flicks through some papers, her phone clamped against her shoulder. The papers concern how Ivan's notes and drafts will be deposited or prepared for publication when he dies, which, the doctors have said, will happen in the near future. Promised? Said.

Anna uses the garlic plate from Provence and the cheese knife from Verona. She puts the food into bowls that have been collected during holidays in Lesbos, Genoa and – the big one for green salads – Helsinki. She puts the bread in a basket from Peru. These objects occupy specific places in Signhildsborg life: this and only this bowl must be used for berries, salad; this knife for rye bread.

Anna sometimes thinks about Ivan's many journeys. She thinks about how it was probably his previous wife who allotted functions to each of these things. She remembers her own things, collected on less exotic holidays.

All trips were more exotic when he was the one travelling. She thinks of this every time she runs the dishwasher and has to fit each object into the intricate hierarchy of the shelves. That he has seen so much and now no longer feels a need to see it again. That none of what she has seen can compare. That he does not mourn the chance to see it all again, with me: that is how far she stretches the thought.

When she talks about cities in Italy, he comments on the density of the traffic there in the seventies. When she mentions that she has read *Danube*, he says he read *Danube* by the Danube and that reading *Danube* by the Danube was wildly overrated, almost a cliché. That Danube/*Danube* is overrated. But I can hardly be angry about that, the way things are, Anna thinks, correcting herself.

Anna knows she is beginning to lose control of her voice. On good days it is calm and melodic as she tells Siri which recipes she has chosen to ensure they fit Siri's restrictive diet, but on bad days it switches too quickly, uncurbed, like a kite plummeting towards the ground when the air has suddenly gone out of it: her own analogy from when the children were small. For fuck's sake! she says, and hears the rings spread out across the water of the empty kitchen.

Anna remembers the first time she experienced the relief of someone slapping her across the face. It was a warm night and there were bats in the air and they frightened her. She was afraid they would get their claws into her hair and never let go. Anna cannot remember the lead-up to the fight, nor is it important. She thinks it was the last summer with someone, so perhaps there was not even a quarrel underlying it, just some unguarded comment, some small error.

When Anna has difficulty sleeping or when she is performing repetitive tasks she sometimes sinks back into that dark, balmy air, down into a wicker chair, down into how she consistently managed to avoid seeing him until he followed her out onto the lawn.

She remembers him grabbing her and hitting her in the face and that it felt momentous. She remembers the way down to the beach with sand beneath her feet.

She remembers being able to feel it, she could feel everything, and then came the remorse and the kisses, all the other things that are nice too, even if they do not have the same potential as a slap.

The carer must feel sorrow for the life that has been short-ened, limited, or that is nearing the end.

The carer must feel frustration: at the inherent injustice of biology, at the overly chilly reception of the doctors or their ingratiating empathy. The carer must fight bureau-cracy and insist upon the best mobility aids.

The carer must not, however, feel frustration towards the person being cared for, or let slip that anything in his behaviour makes the task more challenging than it need be.

The health service provides brochures for loved ones: *Remember to look after yourself too.* It's purely about making savings on social care, says Siri with a snort, opening a window to the April weather. If fewer people cared for their loved ones at home, if fewer people could be bothered, the cost of social care would be through the roof.

But of course I don't mean you, she says to Anna then, when she sees that Anna has heard what she said to her. Of course you have to look after yourself too!

Anna knows it is true, that she cannot fall to pieces in the midst of all this. But Anna cannot carry out the actions generally assumed to be a part of looking after oneself too! She has backed away from the precipice, backed away from her rage in the park, she has managed to rein in her thoughts again.

She cannot book theatre tickets or wonder when she might get out in the woods to pick wild mushrooms. She cannot think about how the price of flights these days has brought a trip to Italy within relatively easy reach, even on one's own, or whether it might be possible to travel to another country altogether. She is locked into respectability. Respectability calls for calm.

As a result of not being allowed to think about what she might do afterwards, she has no need to think about what she will be, which doors will slowly crack open again and what will be on the other side of them, if anything.

She spends the nights awake, bringing glasses of water, pills. She counts them carefully and waits until Ivan falls asleep again. She sits in the chair in case he calls again. She feels an abstract sense of worry that she has given him the wrong dosage, like when she is unsure whether she has turned off the gas.

The pauses between his breaths give her time to fear that he has stopped breathing, before he starts again. Every time she thinks it is time to get up out of the chair, that it is over, he starts breathing again. She sleeps in short bursts. When she wakes, her elbows ache; they are stiff regardless of whether she has been holding something or not.

If she does not want to go through these motions, someone else will. She has no real position from which to negotiate: what she is doing can be done by others. The justification for her existence lies in her not negotiating for remuneration, in the fact that it is not her job to take care of this dying man but that it comes from some inner source.

A paid role would be something else, maybe simpler, but going into that line of work would be an impossibility. If Anna is to clean she must do so for free. Despite the absolute, crystal-clear obviousness of this, she cannot think of any way in which she has made herself indispensable. It is impossible to think that it is once again the grasp of her hands that is indispensable, that it is hands and legs that can walk upstairs and a brain that can remember four numbers and the hand on the gearstick and driving to the pharmacy and consulting on funeral arrangements and double-checking with the doctor. All these things she does, they are not what is indispensable. It must be her, something inside her, that has value. It must be a sign of indispensability, this coming to terms with being the supporting act.

When Anna comes in with the three o'clock tablets, Ivan is sitting there balancing a pen between his ring and index fingers. It is one of his little habits and like all his little habits he once immortalized it in a book: some man in some book got that habit from him, weighing a pen in his hand as he thinks. She knows this, it was one of those things he used to tell her in the early days but has stopped telling her now. That someone else got some other trait and that even the objects here on the desk have been portioned out over the years.

He has stuck them in as greetings to himself, reminders, in the same way he did with the weather, food and the first time Siri was sectioned, he used to say. You change the names of restaurants, the direction of the wind, he said, whether she tried to cut herself or overdosed, and suddenly you've got literature.

I've never spared myself, Ivan said about this. Anna has mentally shelved the words for future use so she can say *All those small gestures of his, they're alive still, and we know he never spared himself, as he said to me right at the end.* Implicit in this will be the suggestion that he never spared her either, that she suffered because of it, that she shouldered that burden.

Regardless, the gestures are still there, in a body, even though it cannot be used for much else. Just now it was the pen between the fingers. The glasses being pushed up and down the nose is the one for the dinner table. He no longer uses his standard phrase when he ejaculates, repetitive, empty after the first evacuation, but he still kneads one foot with the other while he thinks. He still appears to think.

The at-home care team are arriving at 3.15. Anna will not manage to get her work done before that. You only get the care team towards the end, when it is primarily about pain relief.

Siri has jotted down some questions in a notebook, and she asks them. Pain relief, for example, even if it makes Pappa sleep more soundly at night, are there not side effects? I haven't noticed him waking that much and it's important for him to be as clear-headed as possible so he can finish writing his book. My father and I both think that's important. I'm helping him with it a fair bit, she explains to the team.

Anna gets out the bottles of pills. She is unsure whether to offer the visitors coffee, she is uncertain about everything. She has a vague sense they think Ivan is not being cared for properly, or that he is being cared for brilliantly by Siri and they are wondering who Anna is.

Anna's back feels tense and she tells Harry, who calls in the middle of everything, that she doesn't have time to talk right now. The at-home care team talk in low voices with Siri, who is next of kin, about days and weeks and Siri talks about this on the phone with her mother. They discuss things but Anna hears only half the conversation: Siri's voice, which is allowed to be the voice of the child, the sad child who needs consoling.

Ivan lies on the sofa with his feet up to help with the swelling. He is not quite coherent, he is talking about his book, and when it comes to art it is hard to get a sense of what is hallucination, what is creative process, what is masterful and what is an imitation of mastery.

He is not so confused that Anna can comment on his confusion and the possibility that he does not entirely know what he wants. It is important that she does not act as an interpreter, Siri wants to be clear about that. You can't make yourself Pappa's interpreter, she says.

They eat together at the table. Fish soup again, it's a sure bet, variations are easy. This one is without saffron but with lemongrass and a little chilli heat. It is good but Ivan does not want to taste it. ...it's like a conversation... Ivan says, back in his rut. Anna rises to get the cheese. Neither Ivan nor Siri care now whether Anna slices cheese, she is not the one they are talking to. She slices cheese like a child slices cheese at a table for adults, like a waiter slices cheese for their diners.

A conversation, a dialogue, a tonality, he goes on. Anna is not thinking. She asks if anyone else would like bread with their cheese. Bread? With cheese? Siri rolls her eyes but restrains herself. This soup really is delicious, Anna, she says. Then Ivan grows tired and is helped back to his desk again by Anna.

When Ivan is about to lose his balance, she holds him first by the hand, then by the arm; she takes his weight on the stairs. Her joints remember carrying, bearing up, waiting on steps, conveying through her hand that you have to make it all the way up because I cannot make it all the way up with you in my arms and all these bags too.

In the evening Ivan needs to pee again. The bottles are hard white plastic, and there are two of them. She runs them through the dishwasher at regular intervals, otherwise she just rinses them. The easiest thing is for Ivan to sit on the edge of the seat of his walker with her standing to his right. At first it was important for him to undo his trousers himself, but after a few accidents when they did not quite make it she now does it instead.

She unbuckles his belt, the same one he has always had – the leather is worn. Every time she unbuckles it she remembers the time he bound her hands to the bedpost with that belt, but that is just a parenthesis. Then she unbuttons his trousers and takes his penis out of his boxers.

Ivan has to hold on to the handles of the walker so as not to tip forward, so she has to take his penis in her hand, put it into the neck of the bottle, and then hold his penis and the bottle together while he urinates. She feels the bottle growing warm in her hand.

She is leaning forward slightly, which strains her back, a more active tension than the usual one. When he has finished she puts the bottle on the floor – out of the way so they do not kick it over as they go through the three steps: up from the seat, swinging round to the chair, then settling down into it. Sitting in his desk chair, he looks normal.

It is eight o'clock and Anna calls Ivan *darling*, so there can be no doubt she loves him when she gives him his eight o'clock tablets, or afterwards when they tackle the bathroom and everything that occurs in there.

Anna helps Ivan brush his teeth. What a waste, she thinks at times, when the light is falling in a certain way through the window and she is carefully shaving him or combing his hair. What a shame there is no one to see me being good like this. Her arms, the jutting ball of her elbow joint and the bones at her wrists. That no one sees them as they are lowered into the water to wash his hands, that no one can see how the hair falls on her neck as she helps him turn onto his side.

It is a Tuesday, so she cuts his nails. The scissors follow his fingertips, they are so smooth now, unused. She holds his hand and feels the bones, no more than a little bird's. She could bite right through.

Anna massages Ivan with salves, with oil, unscented oil. She massages between his toes and the creases of his groin. She helps him into his pyjamas after the nappy that takes the place of the bottles overnight. It is much larger than the ones familiar from having small children and is constructed differently.

She helps him to his bed and takes the weight as he lies down. Still he grunts. She makes to leave the room to carry on with the work she did not have time for during the day. But he wants her within view; he is not content unless someone is sitting there beside him, humming. It locks her in, and yet it is not a gaze that counts. It affirms nothing but that she fills part of his vision.

Anna sits there, she sits in silence. She cannot bring herself to talk to Ivan, though she knows he can still hear. When she has given everything she has of her hands there is nothing left, there is nothing to say. He lies on the bed and looks at her. She feels no revulsion but she does not have the strength to meet his gaze or talk about the weather, not ever again. Nor can she bring herself to pass on the greetings of people who have called, fewer now and more seldom. What does the weather matter if we never leave this room, she thinks.

While he looks at her, more sleepily now, she toys with the thought of afterwards, at the funeral. That is as far as she dares to go; he is still at the centre of this thought.

Imagining a life in which going to a garden of remembrance or a gravestone is optional, where life can be filled with something other than the walk to the churchyard and waiting for the walk to the churchyard, feels like betrayal.

Imagining the immediate aftermath is not as frightening. She sees it as an extension of her duties: a worthy end for him – the ceremony – is not an act of leaving him behind. Moreover, she likes the thought of that day and its planning, because she will be able to exploit her talent for scenography. They will not have Ivan's portrait propped on some table, nothing as trite as that.

The wake will be in the living room, a friend will be playing the piano. There will not be a priest, of course, but someone will say a few words. Anna is good at these things, she can direct occasions and she knows how to arrange them, like small objects on a desk, an inspiring still life.

She knows too how to lean in profile against a worn cushion and how to pull hairpins from her hair: all the things that come together to make someone want to look at her. The construction of the room and the construction of the woman in it, in the image of the room: artless.

It is pleasant, gentle, to imagine the funeral, a day when she will know how to behave. And yet she cannot quite forget how tired her arms are from lifting, from lowering, from lifting something else. The tension in her back has returned.

He is asleep. The day will soon be over. Anna just needs to finish the ironing, then it will be over. Anna is still ironing Ivan's shirts. She finds it peaceful, it is white laundry in the breeze. Anna thinks while she irons that the shirts are smooth and warm in the iron's wake, like skin beneath her hand. Then she thinks that is a tired metaphor. Anything to do with skin is tired. She feels a degree of pride in knowing that all skin is tired when it comes to language and in the certainty that she would never use metaphors in company.

She irons the shirts even though she knows women should not iron shirts. It's a little different; she is a little different. Anna runs her fingers along the sleeves, opens and closes wardrobes. Anna puts socks in Ivan's drawer.

It is ten o'clock and Anna takes a pack of cigarettes outside and walks along the gravel paths. To and fro. The borders are full of withered remnants at this time of year, at this time of day; the little shoots the spring flowers are sending up are still so small they are hidden in the dusk. It is too dark to walk barefoot; she does not notice until she feels the gravel cutting into the soles of her feet. Her lipstick leaves traces on her cigarette butts despite being invisible on her lips.

The ring falls from her knuckle when she jerks her hand; she hears it fall and bends down to pick it up but does not straighten again. Siri waves from the kitchen window and Anna waves back.

The rain comes, first a few drops, then gradually increasing, cold, but she stays unmoving in the middle of the path, crouching there, unable to do anything else.

Darkness begins to fall. Ivan wakes up, she hears it through the open window. It is time to go back in. He gets his pills. If you calm down and close your eyes, she says, I'll read until you fall asleep. He twists and turns his head on the pillow. The room becomes suffocating.

Anna sits on the edge of the bed. Close your eyes! she says. But Ivan does not want to close his eyes, he wants to talk about the colour of the moon and about some cat. She closes her eyes and waits, feeling the blood rushing back and forth in her nose and behind her eyelids. He quiets eventually but his shoulder is still twitching, he cannot settle.

Anna holds his hand, which is a little cold. How can it be cold under all these blankets? She holds both his wrists. Relax now, close your eyes. She sings and sings and feels the thin child's bones of his palms, a memory: this is not the skeleton of a child but of an emaciated man.

Then she leaves. The remorse sneaks up on her immediately: why did she not let him talk? Why did she not stroke him over the temple? What does that say about her? But the remorse lasts only the few steps to the sofa, because now she hears him call out again, and she is back again, in there, whispering between clenched teeth that he must sleep now, and she holds his shoulders and she holds him still with her weight and bites hard on the pillow beside his head. The cotton tastes of detergent.

Anna's cheeks are throbbing, her heart is hot, her hands itch, her top lip is clammy, she feels her eyes pressing into their sockets. Somewhere in the corner of her eye she sees Ivan grow calm and still. He lies there, perfectly straight, rigid. The tension in her hands slips away, bit by bit, she opens her palms and sees the crescent-shaped pits made by her nails, dark in the glow of the night light.

She strokes his hair, his cheek, with hands that have also grown cold. She straightens the covers, she turns his pillow so the cool side faces up. She lies down beside him, holds him and hums slowly. Through the gap in the curtain she sees the April sky grown completely dark.

You know how much I love... she whispers when he is asleep, as though he could still acknowledge her. She runs her fingers along his jaw, the hollow of his throat, his nose. She brushes the thin hair back from his brow.

She gives him more pills and sits beside him and shushes quietly, quieting him until he sleeps again. The laundry flutters behind her eyelids.

When Ivan wakes in the middle of the night, she is so kind. She gets out more pain relief and sleeping pills, what difference can it make? She strokes him on the back, he asks nothing and she says nothing. She lies there listening to the rain on the roof.

When everything that will happen has happened, the woman folds the shirts that remain and puts them in boxes.

At the funeral she moves around the coffin; this is the point against which one is defined. When the coffin too has been removed, she is without contours.

It is impossible to place the undefined in a conversation or at a table. Therefore, it is at this point that the narrative ends. If other events take place, they are undocumented.

STEVNS TRANSLATION PRIZE
Peirene Press | Two Lines Press

The Stevns Translation Prize, run by Peirene Press (UK) and Two Lines Press (US), was launched in 2018 to support emerging literary translators.

Open to all translators who have not yet translated a full-length work of fiction, this annual award rewards great translation and creates new pathways into the profession.

The winner receives a commission to translate a text selected by Peirene Press and Two Lines Press, a six-week retreat in the French Pyrenees, including travel costs, and a dedicated, one-on-one mentorship throughout the translation process.

The Stevns Translation Prize opens for submissions in October and focuses on a different language every year.

With thanks to Martha Stevns, without whom this prize would not be possible.

THE PEIRENE SUBSCRIPTION

Since 2011, Peirene Press has run a subscription service which has brought a world of translated literature to thousands of readers. We seek out great stories and original writing from across the globe, and work with the best translators to bring these books into English – before sending each one to our subscribers ahead of publication. All of our books are beautifully designed collectible paperback editions, printed in the UK using sustainable materials.

Join our reading community today and subscribe to receive three or six books a year, as well as invitations to events and launch parties and discounts on all our titles. We also offer a gift subscription, so you can share your literary discoveries with friends and family.

A one-year subscription costs £38 for three books, or £68 for six books. Postage costs apply.

www.peirenepress.com/subscribe

'The foreign literature specialist'

The Sunday Times

'A class act'

The Guardian